PENGUIN BOOKS

2130

AN ASPIDISTRA IN BABYLON

H. E. BATES

Born in 1905, H. E. Bates was educated at Kettering Grammar School and worked as a journalist before publishing his first book, *The Two Sisters*, when he was twenty. In the next fifteen years he won a distinguished reputation for his stories about English country life. In 1941, as 'Flying Officer X', he wrote his two famous books of short stories – *The Greatest People in the World* and *How Sleep the Brave* – which were followed in 1944 by *Fair Stood the Wind for France*. These, and his subsequent novels of Burma, *The Purple Plain* and *The Jacaranda Tree*, and of India, *The Scarlet Sword*, were highly successful in Britain and America, and have been translated into fifteen foreign languages. His writing took a new direction in 1958 with the appearance of *The Darling Buds of May*, the first of the popular Larkin family novels, which was followed by *A Breath of French Air*, *When the Green Woods Laugh*, and *Oh! To be in England* (1963).

An Aspidistra in Babylon

FOUR NOVELLAS BY
H. E. BATES

PENGUIN BOOKS
In association with Michael Joseph

Penguin Books Ltd, Harmondsworth, Middlesex, England
Penguin Books Pty Ltd, Ringwood, Victoria, Australia

—

First published by Michael Joseph 1960
Published in Penguin Books 1964

—

Copyright © Evensford Productions Ltd, 1960

—

Made and printed in Great Britain
by Cox and Wyman Ltd,
London, Reading, and Fakenham
Set in Monotype Bembo

Contents

An Aspidistra in Babylon

NEARLY forty years ago, when I was a young girl and my mother, a widow, kept a small boarding-house at one end of the sea-front the houses there ran in a sparkling crescent of white and cream under the massive shoulder of chalk cliff on which the castle and its garrison stands. From a distance the castle still looks like an enormous bastion of pumice-coloured flint. By contrast, in those days, the curving line of houses always looked like a freshly starched collar, intensely stiff and respectable, against the strip of biscuit-coloured shingle and the sea.

A great deal of this, I must point out, has changed now. During the war bombs ripped out the entire centre of the collar and you can still see the dirty scars made by shells on the grassy slopes above the town. But two things remain exactly as they were when I lived with my mother there and, in the long blistering summer of 1921, when I was eighteen, I first met an officer in the Guards, a man of forty, named Captain Archie Blaine.

The first thing that has never changed at all is the castle itself. It has the imperishable and inviolate air that belongs to great churches and high mountains. But sometimes, especially on rainy days, it also looks like a prison. At other times something about the particular arrangement of the battlements gives it the appearance of a great clenched granite fist, fingers perpendicular, threatening the sea. The other thing about the town that remains unchanged is far less spectacular. It is, perhaps, even rather trivial, though it may be its very triviality that makes it stick in my mind.

It is simply that all the chimney pots on the houses remaining in the crescent are a very bright, impossible canary yellow. They are also unusually tall and as they stand there above the roofs in blocks of six, eight or even a dozen they have exactly the appearance of lofty organ pipes. You fully expect them to start playing solemn tunes. Of course nothing of the kind ever happens and the only sound you ever hear from them is the greedy squawks of the many huge hungry sea-gulls that sit on them and, by some curious trick of light, or perhaps because the pots are that quite impossible yellow, often look like gross blue owls.

Speaking of this curious trick of colour, I have now remembered a third thing that never changes. It is the extraordinary light that, whenever the sun shines, hangs above the crescent, the castle, the chalk cliffs, the harbour, the sea-walls and the sea. It is not that it is merely of a strikingly pure candescence. It seems actually to leap in air. In some curious way it is uncannily transcendent. It seems to lift you off the ground.

On very hot days, when the chalk of the cliffs looks more naked than usual and there is the faintest ripple on the sea, it has still another quality. It suddenly robs your eyes of the power of focus.

It was on just such a day of naked, blinding light, in June, that I first met Captain Blaine.

2

Of course in a garrison town the one consistently unsurprising thing is to meet a soldier. They are naturally everywhere. You can't escape them. The rankers come into town to drink beer, eat fish and chips and get off with girls. The officers, less evident simply because there are fewer of them, come in to drink at the better hotels or have occasional dinner parties, mostly on Saturdays. The rankers get very drunk and rowdy and fight among themselves when they can't find marines or sailors to fight with, which isn't very often. The officers also get very drunk and are finally carried home up the hill, in their own exclusive fashion, in taxi-cabs. The fights, especially with marines, are apt to be rather bloody.

Nearly forty years ago there were also, of course, many more pubs to get drunk in than there are now. Soldiers, too, were soldiers, not mere conscripted cyphers serving a couple of reluctant years and wearing luminous socks and drain-pipe trousers in off-duty hours. They were cast in Kipling's belching, bawdy mould. They were what Rupert Brooke calls somewhere 'loud and black of mouth' and their women weren't much better.

Small wonder, I suppose, that my mother had her own special name for that brawling soldiers' town.

'Babylon,' she called it. 'That Babylon. Keep away from that Babylon,' she always said to me. 'Don't ever go near that Babylon.'

When you add to all this the fact that ships from the continent were coming into the harbour every day, regularly bringing French and Belgian sailors ashore or foreign visitors on a ten-hour excursion spree, you would naturally come to the conclusion that the town, whatever else it might be, was never dull. You would naturally think also that in that robust male Babylon a girl of eighteen wouldn't have much difficulty in getting herself noticed, taken out or even made a fuss of by a man.

Both conclusions would be very wrong. To me, at least until that blistering eventful summer of 1921, it was never anything but infinitely and terribly dull. It was so dull that I couldn't even hate it. Today I think it a very pretty, charming town, full of colouring and bristling with a certain character. In those days it was just a smudge on the shore.

As to the men, the soldiers and all the rest, I simply didn't exist for them. This is not entirely surprising, however, since I was clearly infinitely and terribly dull myself. The best description of myself that I can think of is to say that I was as dull as one of the many aspidistras that cluttered up the rooms, the hallway and even the dining tables of our little boarding-house. I was just that – a female aspidistra and nothing more.

For example I had, until my seventeenth year, worn my hair down my back in a long thick plait tied with a large plain black ribbon. It was rather greasy hair, dark and unwaved, of the kind that most women struggle frantically to alter or at all costs to disguise. I just wasn't aware of it. When I looked in the mirror I saw it simply as a frame for a rather narrow paste-coloured face in which the dark brown eyes were too large and consequently much out of proportion. Naturally I wore no make-up either, so that my forehead and my rather high cheek-bones always shone very soapily.

The one thing about myself I might have claimed as not being dull was my figure. My body was slender but very smooth and without a single blemish except a perfectly circular brown mole, rather large, between my left breast and my shoulder. But since no one except myself ever saw my body or caught even the faintest glimpse of the mole it really wasn't very important to me. I ought to add here that although my legs were really quite shapely I naturally wore black woollen stockings.

My mother wore black stockings too. In fact she wore nothing but black, continuously. Mourning for my father, who had died ten years before, had become a habit. Widow-hood was a cross to be serenely and, when possible, silently borne.

I must refrain from being unjust to my mother, especially as what happened to me that summer was not really of her making, but she was a woman who had life neatly summed up in a series of catch-phrases, all of them fallacies.

Her favourite among these was 'If you trust other people they will trust you.' Second only to this, I fancy, was 'If you don't want people to think ill of you don't begin by thinking ill of them.' Under such fallacious guidance, delivered in her mournful, rather monotonous voice, all individuality in me had died. I was dull only because I was fearful of doing anything opposed to these apparently solemn truths of hers.

Ruby is an illustration of this curious and important business. Ruby was one of our chambermaids, a generously-built, good-looking, juicy girl of twenty-eight or so with reddish hair and half-dissolute grey-green eyes that always looked much older than the rest of her. I liked Ruby and I have good cause to remember, and be grateful for, those half-dissolute, old-looking eyes.

On her days off Ruby was, in fact, part of that Babylon my mother always warned me so much about. She was the good time free-and-easy, the soldiers' friend.

'Over-affectionate, duckie, that's me. Give, give, that's my trouble. Never know when to stop. Ought to think about settling down. Never will, though.'

I very much liked going into the maids' room, behind the kitchen, and talking to Ruby, or even upstairs to her room, where we could be alone. Chambermaids didn't have luxuries like bathrooms in those days and sometimes I went into her bedroom and caught her having what she called a strip-wash, bare to the waist, over her marble wash-stand.

'Come in, duckie. Sit on the bed. Don't mind me. Up as far as possible and down as far as possible. Got to get the muck off today somehow. Only had a cat-lick yesterday.'

Ruby's ripe and infectious laugh always bounced about the bedroom as generously as her big breasts swung above the soapy water as she bent to wash them.

I not only liked Ruby; I was fascinated by her. I was also, I confess, sometimes a little horrified. I was horrified, for instance, when I caught her washing one day and found her back and shoulders scored with a sickly mass of black and yellow bruises.

'Ruby,' I said. 'Your back! Whatever happened? Whatever on earth did you do?'

Ruby, far from being concerned, merely filled the bedroom with her customary ripe and careless laughter.

'Bit of love, duckie, that's all. They get taken a bit fierce like that sometimes.'

'You mean a man did it? You mean you actually –'

Ruby pealed with laughter again.

'Oh! that's all right, duckie,' she said. 'That's a good sign, that is. You know they got it bad then. Know they really feel about you.'

My mother's counsel of putting yourself into other people's places, under other people's skins, didn't work out very well that day. Try as I would I couldn't get under Ruby's handsome, dissolute skin and imagine myself being beaten black and yellow for love and what Elizabeth Barratt Browning called 'for love's sake only'.

Two days after this revealing occurrence it was Ruby's afternoon off. After lunch had been served my mother was taking her usual hour's rest in her bedroom. I was in our private sitting-room, alone, reading verse, which as you've probably gathered I liked to do. Verse, in fact, was the only thing through which, ever so remotely, I came near to finding myself. I had naturally gleaned all I knew of love from what I read in verse.

That afternoon, I remember, was extraordinarily hot and still, without a single breath of breeze across the harbour, and it must have been at its hottest when, about half past three, one of the other maids tapped on the door, came in and said:

'Sorry to disturb you, Miss Christine, but your mother's sound asleep and I don't like to wake her. Can you come a minute? There's an officer here who says he'd like to speak to you. A Captain Blaine.'

When I am reading I have a curious habit of tucking one foot under me and sitting on it. After a time the foot either goes to sleep or gets stiff and twisted so that when I get up I find myself temporarily off balance, walking for the next half minute or so as if I'd sprained my ankle.

This is how I went out to make my first acquaintance with Captain Blaine. I imagine I must have looked pretty silly as I hobbled into the hallway, which incidentally was paved with those cold and slippery Italian mosaic tiles which were so fashionable years ago and the result was that the first thing the Captain did was to take a swift and inquiring look at my legs.

'I'm so sorry. I hope I haven't disturbed you?' he said. 'Have you hurt your foot?'

With a rush of diffidence I blushed and assured him I hadn't. I'd merely sat on it.

He gave a short engaging chuckle.

'Really?' he said. 'I always thought legs were for standing on?'

'Oh! that's just me,' I said. I tried to speak coolly as a means of suppressing my growing shyness. 'I like to be different.'

For the second time he gave that engaging chuckle of his. At the same time he shot another quick and inquiring glance at me. His face was also turned towards the sea, so that for a moment or two the reflected light of it, with that curious blinding power I have already tried to describe, was full in his eyes.

They were eyes of a very remarkable and liquid quality of blueness. If I describe them as being without depth it will perhaps convey the impression that they were shallow. On the contrary they were extraordinarily subtle. They were like the petals of certain sorts of flowers that appear at first glance to be merely of a single, solid colour and then suddenly prove to be excitingly iridescent.

What made them still more arresting was that they were uncommonly cool, not to say glacial, in that awfully hot afternoon, and that they were set in a face that in all other respects

13

was very dark – dark brows, dark chin and jowls, dark guards-man's moustache and rather fine dark nostrils.

'Terribly remiss of me,' he said suddenly. 'Didn't introduce myself. Blaine.' His officer's cap was tucked with military correctness under one arm. The uniform was a bluish-grey, a sort of pigeon colour, high in the collar. Magnificently band-box, the whole thing. 'I called to inquire about a room.'

He gave that engaging chuckle again and signalled vivid assurances with iridescent eyes.

'Oh! not for myself. I'm up at the castle. Quarters there. No,' he said, 'it's for an aunt of mine. She's a shade shaky. Asthma – heart gets strained.'

'When would you want the room?' I said. 'For how long?'

'Depends. Might be a long time. Might be very short.' He gave a sort of resigned shrug of the shoulders. 'Never really tell, with this heart thing. It's dry here. She's been living in the West Country – far too damp for her. I thought if I got her here – one never knows. Might hang on for years.'

Was she really an invalid? I asked. My mother didn't like invalids about the place and nor did the maids. In fact they were all rather against the tyranny of long lets.

'Oh! no,' he said. 'Far from it. Very spry. Even gads about a bit.'

I hardly knew what to say. I started to explain to him that I could do nothing without asking my mother but that she was asleep and I didn't want to wake her.

He was at once all charm and solicitude.

'Oh! don't give it a thought. Wouldn't dream of letting you wake her. Certainly not. I can come back. When would it be convenient to see her?'

I suggested that evening, perhaps about six, and he said:

'Admirable. Couldn't be better. I'll trot along then.'

He turned to go and then suddenly paused at the open door of the hallway. The smell of sea and seaweed was very strong in the hot calm air and the brass curb of the doorstep shone like a

...n't occur to him to apologize for being late, for
...ason that he was one of those people to whom
...lly other people's time, means absolutely nothing –
...al. Not chronically bad, you understand. But
... it brings on bronchial relapses. It's hard on the

...e time I kept watching those captivating iridescent
...aiting for a sign of recognition and all the while
...are of the reason for their inability to focus me.

...ds quiet and a dry climate. That's why I want to get
...And particularly in your boarding house, because it's
... end of the promenade and she has the lawns and
... just opposite. She can be really quiet here.'

...e need extra attention, any nursing or anything of
...ny mother asked.

...atever. None whatever. Absolutely none. Per-
...le of looking after herself. It's just the occasional
...threat, that's all. Otherwise she'll be perfectly con-
...her reading, her bit of crochet and so on. And two or
...ons a week I'll run her along the coast in the car.'
...as of course nothing very difficult or complicated
... this and soon my mother and Captain Blaine were
...erms. Miss Charlesworth would arrive during the
...eek-end. He would meet her at the station. And if
... she would stay for at least the rest of the summer
...much longer.

...at, madam, and thank you,' he said to my mother,
...y obliged,' and at last departed with that over-
...f his that had me utterly and completely fooled.
...a great sickening stupid lump in my throat when
...ut somehow I managed to say:
...ou think of him? Did you like him?'
...o much,' my mother said. That was all. 'He

...rt of cold blackness came over me. If my

strip of fire. A channel steamer coming in stern first across the harbour was making smoke and the cloud of it was the only blemish on the blinding purity of the day.

'I do hope we can fix things up,' he said. 'Sort of duty to see that she's all right, if you know what I mean. I'm her only relative. Must do the best for her.'

He flashed another winning blue signal at me with those remarkable eyes of his and then stared at the steamer crossing the harbour, at the same time giving the briefest sigh.

'What a day to be crossing. What a thought, eh? Get the Blue Train from Paris tonight and in Nice tomorrow. What about that?'

The fact that the question was purely rhetorical didn't prevent my saying an abysmally stupid thing.

'I don't know. Where's Nice?' I said.

He was quick to seize on this piece of idiotic innocence of mine and said:

'You've never heard of Nice? Now that I just won't believe.'

'Truly,' I said.

'Just won't, just can't and just don't believe.'

Suddenly, for the second time, I felt myself flushing and once again I was completely hypnotized by that remarkably charming, iridescent stare of his.

'Just isn't possible,' he said. 'You're pulling my leg.'

'Oh! but it is,' I assured him. 'It is. I wouldn't dream of saying something I didn't mean.'

Perhaps it sounds a little exaggerated but that intensely naïve remark of mine was perhaps the most important thing I ever said to Captain Blaine. If I had stripped myself stark naked on the doorstep in the blinding sunshine I could hardly have revealed more of myself to him.

'I suppose you've been there very often?' I said. 'Is it wonderful?'

'Practically lived there before the war. Couldn't tear myself away. Wine three francs a bottle. Wonderful? It's divine. It's celestial. If you can imagine heaven mating with paradise Nice would be their daughter.'

This slightly extravagant turn of phrase both amused and captivated me. I laughed aloud.

'It sounds marvellous,' I said. 'I shall have to start saving all my pennies and get there.'

'Ah! the pennies, the pennies,' he said. He actually gave me a brief, reassuring, friendly pinch on the arm. 'The pennies. You've hit it now, girl. There's the rub. Plenty of pennies, that's the snag. That's the form. That's what you must have.'

He gave an almost sorrowful shake of the head, at the same time chuckling again. A moment later he put on his cap, shook me by the hand and saluted.

'Good-bye. Charmed to meet you. Back at six.'

He crossed the road to where a small dark red coupé was parked in the blazing sun and I stood for a minute longer at the doorway, watching him crank it up, get into it and, after a careless wave of the hand to me, drive it away.

As it disappeared along the promenade that old trick of light played itself on me again. But this time I was more than dazzled by it. For quite some seconds I was almost blind.

Of course it just isn't possible to capture an entire personality in one short meeting, however much you may delude yourself you may have done so, and my experience with Captain Blaine that afternoon was very comparable to what I have at times experienced with certain kinds of flowers.

I am referring more particularly to flowers that are strongly perfumed: carnations, roses, lilies, and so on. My experience has often been that in the first rapturous moment of burying your face in their petals you really seem to drink in perfume in one great exquisite liquid draught. But only a few seconds later, when you seek to repeat the experience, you are doomed to disappointment. For some reason the perfume is no longer there. In that first eager rush of thirst you seem to have drained

the petals dry. The flower is tempo...
is dead.

This was very much my experience...
our second meeting that day. All that...
was full of Captain Blaine. I suppose I...
sitting room until nearly six o'clock, trying...
read verse and yet never managing to focus a...
the time I was as powerfully and keenly awar...
as if the room had been full of flowers. In the hot...
I kept drinking and drinking him in.

Perhaps I'm not putting all this in the best possib...
what I am trying to say is that I wanted to repe...
delicious and exciting experience in exactly its or...
when Captain Blaine came back at six o'clock. I...
with a flower, to re-experience that first divine de...
the perfume.

And, as with a flower, I was disappointed.

There may have been several reasons for this. I...
place Captain Blaine was very late in arriving. It w...
nearly eight o'clock before he arrived. This, as...
covered, was quite typical of him and afterwar...
surprised me.

In the second place he was slightly ...nk. This...
innocence, I didn't appreciate at the ti...
standably, since when Archie Blaine was...
disgusting, obvious, tedious way bu...
stiffening up of the entire muscular sy...
anything more correct than ever.

The third reason, I think, was th...
As I have tried to indicate she alwa...
something other than myself bu...
than myself. And that evening I ...
strongly. I was effaced; I simpl...
Captain Blaine hardly took the...

'My aunt, Miss Charleswor...

strip of fire. A channel steamer coming in stern first across the harbour was making smoke and the cloud of it was the only blemish on the blinding purity of the day.

'I do hope we can fix things up,' he said. 'Sort of duty to see that she's all right, if you know what I mean. I'm her only relative. Must do the best for her.'

He flashed another winning blue signal at me with those remarkable eyes of his and then stared at the steamer crossing the harbour, at the same time giving the briefest sigh.

'What a day to be crossing. What a thought, eh? Get the Blue Train from Paris tonight and in Nice tomorrow. What about that?'

The fact that the question was purely rhetorical didn't prevent my saying an abysmally stupid thing.

'I don't know. Where's Nice?' I said.

He was quick to seize on this piece of idiotic innocence of mine and said:

'You've never heard of Nice? Now that I just won't believe.'

'Truly,' I said.

'Just won't, just can't and just don't believe.'

Suddenly, for the second time, I felt myself flushing and once again I was completely hypnotized by that remarkably charming, iridescent stare of his.

'Just isn't possible,' he said. 'You're pulling my leg.'

'Oh! but it is,' I assured him. 'It is. I wouldn't dream of saying something I didn't mean.'

Perhaps it sounds a little exaggerated but that intensely naïve remark of mine was perhaps the most important thing I ever said to Captain Blaine. If I had stripped myself stark naked on the doorstep in the blinding sunshine I could hardly have revealed more of myself to him.

'I suppose you've been there very often?' I said. 'Is it wonderful?'

'Practically lived there before the war. Couldn't tear myself away. Wine three francs a bottle. Wonderful? It's divine. It's celestial. If you can imagine heaven mating with paradise Nice would be their daughter.'

This slightly extravagant turn of phrase both amused and captivated me. I laughed aloud.

'It sounds marvellous,' I said. 'I shall have to start saving all my pennies and get there.'

'Ah! the pennies, the pennies,' he said. He actually gave me a brief, reassuring, friendly pinch on the arm. 'The pennies. You've hit it now, girl. There's the rub. Plenty of pennies, that's the snag. That's the form. That's what you must have.'

He gave an almost sorrowful shake of the head, at the same time chuckling again. A moment later he put on his cap, shook me by the hand and saluted.

'Good-bye. Charmed to meet you. Back at six.'

He crossed the road to where a small dark red coupé was parked in the blazing sun and I stood for a minute longer at the doorway, watching him crank it up, get into it and, after a careless wave of the hand to me, drive it away.

As it disappeared along the promenade that old trick of light played itself on me again. But this time I was more than dazzled by it. For quite some seconds I was almost blind.

Of course it just isn't possible to capture an entire personality in one short meeting, however much you may delude yourself you may have done so, and my experience with Captain Blaine that afternoon was very comparable to what I have at times experienced with certain kinds of flowers.

I am referring more particularly to flowers that are strongly perfumed: carnations, roses, lilies, and so on. My experience has often been that in the first rapturous moment of burying your face in their petals you really seem to drink in perfume in one great exquisite liquid draught. But only a few seconds later, when you seek to repeat the experience, you are doomed to disappointment. For some reason the perfume is no longer there. In that first eager rush of thirst you seem to have drained

the petals dry. The flower is temporarily exhausted.
is dead.

This was very much my experience with Captai
our second meeting that day. All that hot afterm
was full of Captain Blaine. I suppose I must hav
sitting room until nearly six o'clock, trying as I so
read verse and yet never managing to focus a single
the time I was as powerfully and keenly aware of
as if the room had been full of flowers. In the hot Ju
I kept drinking and drinking him in.

Perhaps I'm not putting all this in the best possibl
what I am trying to say is that I wanted to repe
delicious and exciting experience in exactly its or
when Captain Blaine came back at six o'clock.
with a flower, to re-experience that first divine d
the perfume.

And, as with a flower, I was disappointed.

There may have been several reasons for this. I
place Captain Blaine was very late in arriving. It
nearly eight o'clock before he arrived. This, as
covered, was quite typical of him and afterw
surprised me.

In the second place he was slightly drunk
nnocence, I didn't appreciate at the time and qu
ndably, since when Archie Blaine was drunk it was never in a
gusting, obvious, tedious way but only in an apparent
ffening up of the entire muscular system, so that he looked if
nything more correct than ever.

The third reason, I think, was the presence of my mother.
As I have tried to indicate she always made me feel not merely
something other than myself but something very much less
than myself. And that evening I not only felt her influence very
strongly. I was effaced; I simply wasn't there. And as a result
Captain Blaine hardly took the trouble to look or speak to me.

'My aunt, Miss Charlesworth,' he explained to my mother –

lidn't occur to him to apologize for being late, for
reason that he was one of those people to whom
ally other people's time, means absolutely nothing –
al. Not chronically bad, you understand. But
it brings on bronchial relapses. It's hard on the

e time I kept watching those captivating iridescent
aiting for a sign of recognition and all the while
are of the reason for their inability to focus me.
ds quiet and a dry climate. That's why I want to get
nd particularly in your boarding house, because it's
t end of the promenade and she has the lawns and
just opposite. She can be really quiet here.'
e need extra attention, any nursing or anything of
ny mother asked.
atever. None whatever. Absolutely none. Per-
le of looking after herself. It's just the occasional
threat, that's all. Otherwise she'll be perfectly con-
her reading, her bit of crochet and so on. And two or
ons a week I'll run her along the coast in the car.'
s of course nothing very difficult or complicated
is and soon my mother and Captain Blaine were
s. Miss Charlesworth would arrive during the
week-end. He would meet her at the station. And i
all went well she would stay for at least the rest of the summ
and perhaps much longer.

'Goodnight, madam, and thank you,' he said to my moth
'most awfully obliged,' and at last departed with that ove
stiff bearing of his that had me utterly and completely fooled.

There was a great sickening stupid lump in my throat when
he had gone but somehow I managed to say:

'What did you think of him? Did you like him?'

'He talks too much,' my mother said. That was all. 'He
talks too much.'

An awful sort of cold blackness came over me. If my

mother had said outright, in the plainest and most unequivocal of terms, that she thought Captain Blaine was nothing more than an evil and corrupting influence I couldn't have been more outraged. I just turned and rushed madly upstairs and lay there for the rest of the evening in the bed, beating my hands in dark hatred on the counterpane.

Women, nevertheless, have strange intuitions about men. They possess an uncanny curious sixth sense about them. They also have, of course, their blindnesses and that day my mother divined something about Captain Blaine that it took me almost the rest of that year to discover.

Where I had detected in the air, in my thirsty adolescent eagerness, only perfumes and charms and iridescence, only the dazzle of summer, my mother had already seen a cloud.

3

Miss Charlesworth duly arrived on the following Saturday afternoon, dutifully fetched from the station by Captain Blaine in the little red coupé.

'Bertie dear,' was Captain Blaine's affectionate way of addressing her. 'Bertie dear.'

She was a tallish, rather angular woman of seventy whose face, under its crimped white hair, had the appearance of being made of pinkish-mauve enamel that had got rather dusty. She was in fact very much over-powdered, just as she was also very much over-dressed, in a very lacy kind of way, and over-jewelled and over-trunked.

In all I think she brought with her seven or eight large travelling trunks that day. She also had a great deal of subsidiary paraphernalia in the way of parasols, umbrellas, walking sticks, clocks, reticules, sewing-bags, jewel cases and that sort of thing. I fully expected her also to produce either pince-nez or lorgnettes or both, but in fact she did nothing of the kind, and for a very good reason.

Her large grey eyes were as sharp and apparently youthful as my own. She had no need of glasses.

Ruby, who had a quick knack of summing-up the foibles, oddities, and shortcomings of guests both male and female, at once called her the Duchess.

'Couldn't have more clothes, anyway, duckie, even if she was,' she said to me. 'Twenty-three dresses I counted in the wardrobe this morning. And four jewel cases. Worth a bob or two I should say.'

It duly became apparent, as Captain Blaine had suggested, that Miss Charlesworth, for all her appearance of excessive fussiness, was going to be, as a guest, of little or no bother to us. She clearly belonged to that race of gentlefolk who, though never having to work, are highly self-sufficient. They are monuments of busyness.

Miss Charlesworth in fact, read a great deal, crocheted and knitted a great deal, played patience a great deal and wrote, every morning between eleven and one, great quantities of letters.

It was one of these letters that brought me my next meeting with Captain Blaine. One brilliant morning in early July Miss Charlesworth rang the bell in the writing-room and asked the answering parlourmaid if she could see my mother.

'I'm most anxious to get a note to my nephew at the garrison,' she explained, 'and I wondered if one of the maids could take it.'

My mother, apologizing, proceeded to explain that it was exceedingly difficult to spare one of the girls at that time of day and why didn't Miss Charlesworth telephone?

The answer was typical.

'I dislike telephones,' Miss Charlesworth said. 'In fact I distrust them. They lack privacy. What I have to say to Captain Blaine is confidential.'

At this moment I went past the writing-room door on my way to the kitchen and it prompted my mother to say:

'I'm sure Christine would take it, however. Wouldn't you, Christine? A note for Captain Blaine?'

'Deliver it to him personally, child,' Miss Charlesworth said. 'Personally. Remember – I trust you.'

As I walked up the long curving road to the castle just after two o'clock that afternoon it was very hot. The high, white cliffs glared with an almost savage light above the sea and although I had put on the coolest and lightest of dresses, a simple pale cream shantung, I felt awfully nervous and clammy. I was nervous because I could foresee some difficulty in finding Captain Blaine, for the simple reason that although from a distance the castle looks no more than a single solid block of masonry it is in fact almost a little town. It is a positive labyrinth up there of streets, squares, terraces of houses, quarters, stables, armouries, and heaven knows what.

And then, almost at the top of the hill, when I was already within sight of the sentry boxes at the gates, I had a stroke of luck. I heard a car changing gear on the hill behind me and when I turned to look at it I saw that familiar dark red coupé, with the hood down, and in it Captain Blaine.

As it went past me I waved Miss Charlesworth's envelope and shouted. Twenty yards farther on the car stopped and I started running.

Even on the hottest days there is always an uplift of breeze on that hill and as I ran forward a sudden light whirl of wind caught at my big-brimmed white straw hat and lifted the shantung skirt above my knees.

I was still trying to hold down hat and skirt when I reached Captain Blaine, who stared at me with those iridescent eyes dancing with astonishment.

'Good God, girl, I didn't know you.'

'I've got a note for you,' I said, panting slightly, 'from Miss Charlesworth.'

'Awfully, awfully sorry,' he said. 'Really didn't know you. You look different somehow.'

I was foolish enough, believe it or not, to ask 'How?'

'Don't know.' He sat there in the driving seat looking at me quizzically, all charm. 'Must be the dress. No it isn't. I know. It's the hat. I've never seen you in a hat before.'

I flushed. It's always the little things that get women. It's always the stupid little trivialities that trap them.

'Makes you look older. More mature.'

'Oh! really?'

As if he hadn't already said enough to have me in helpless enslavement he suddenly smiled and said, with bland enchantment:

'You suit the day. You look like a bit of sunlight blown up from the sea.'

Could any girl, I ask you, want more than that? I lapped up these blandishments as a kitten laps up warm new milk.

'Oh! the note,' I said, giggling slightly. 'I was forgetting the note. It was a bit of luck seeing you like this. Miss Charlesworth said to be sure to give you the note personally. She trusted me to do that, she said.'

A sharp change came over his face. He even ignored the note in his penetrating eagerness to make quite sure what I had said.

'She said what?'

'She said she trusted me.'

A smile crept back so slowly to his face that its final rest there gave it a look of quite innocent astonishment.

'Do you know you've just said something very remarkable?' he said.

'Me?' I said and I giggled nervously again. 'How?'

'My aunt has never trusted anyone in her life,' he said. 'Not a soul.'

By this time he had put the note in his pocket and I stood there for some seconds with nothing to say, aware only of the sun flashing on the bonnet of the car, his tunic buttons and far below us on the surface of the sea.

'You saw all that paraphernalia she brought?' he said. 'That's an example of how little she trusts people. That's her all, in those damn trunks. Lugs it all from place to place, wherever she goes, like a camel train. She wouldn't trust a fly.'

It is hardly necessary, I imagine, to say how all this affected me. It was like being told that you, in a whole flock of sparrows, have really turned out, after all, to be nothing less than a golden oriole.

'Most remarkable thing I ever heard,' he said. 'You must be an extraordinary person. Can't believe it – Bertie *trusting* you.'

The barely visible line of summer horizon seemed to tilt as another rise of breeze caught my hat and lifted it up, half sideways, from my face.

'Had lunch?' he said.

'Oh! yes,' I said. 'But I suppose you haven't, have you? Please don't let me keep you.'

'Never have any, not when it's so hot,' he said. 'Get a pretty square breakfast and then carry through to dinner. Always got to do the dinner anyway. Can't escape that. Mess tradition, the colonel and that sort of thing.'

He opened the door of the car.

'Hop in. I'll drive you back. Come to that, I'll drive you anywhere.' He smiled in that marvellously iridescent way of his, full into my eyes. 'Game? What say?'

What indeed could I say? My grasp of the next few succeeding moments was so vague that I actually forgot, as we whirled round the high corner beyond the castle, to hold on to my hat With a whistling explosion it blew off my head and landed in the back seat and my hair started flowing in the wind.

I suppose he must have asked me at least a dozen times where I would like to be driven that afternoon before I really woke up to a clear realization of what was going on.

'Tea somewhere? Along the coast?' He was voluble and gay. 'Where's the nearest lighthouse?'

'Oh! I hate lighthouses. They give me a queer feeling in my legs,' I said, laughing. 'No, no – inland. Let's go inland.'

Suddenly I knew where I wanted to go.

'Do you know the forest?' I said. 'It's about six or seven miles from here. You turn off at a mill. I often go out there, especially in spring. It's full of primroses in spring. They're the nearest primroses to the sea.'

I often think that women who wear their hair short never really know that wonderful feeling of liquid exhilaration that comes from having a warm wind blow like water through hair that is really long.

There is no other sensation quite like it in the world and by the time we had reached the outskirts of beech and oak and sweet chestnut that make up the forest I was in a state of breathless, half-orgiastic delight.

'Well, this is my forest,' I said.

When Captain Blaine finally pulled up the car at a point where the trees almost met overhead, we were in a sort of deep green tunnel, wonderfully cool, without sunshine.

'Your forest? Yours?'

'That's how I always think of it,' I said. 'Nobody else ever comes here anyway. Not a soul.'

'Until today.'

I wasn't sure at that moment whether he was teasing me or not. He got out of the car and came round to my side of it, holding the door open for me. In that exhilarating rush across the hills I had quite forgotten all about my appearance and when he opened the door there suddenly was my skirt, blown half-way above my knees, showing an inch or two of bare thigh above the stockings.

But somehow it didn't worry me and with a giggle I jumped down from the car and said:

'Oh! that was the most terrific, terrific drive. Divine. My head's going round and round and round.'

'What shall we do?' he said.

'Let's walk,' I said. 'I'll show you a place where the beech-leaves lie about a yard thick, even in summer. I call it the place of the everlasting leaves.'

If Captain Archie Blaine regarded these outpourings as so much adolescent saccharine he never revealed it by a single word, a smile or the flicker of an eye. In fact he actually seemed to be so much in sympathy with them that he suddenly took my hand. As he did so I felt a cool new thrill go through me from my thighs to my hair and a moment later I started half running through the forest, through shadow hardly ever broken by sunlight, to that secret beech-leaf altar of mine where from time to time I thought nothing of lying and dreaming half a day away.

When we got there I lay down in the deep dry leaves, as I always liked to do, and he took off his tunic and lay there with me.

We talked a bit, I quite forget what about now, but presently the conversation got round, as it was always to do sooner or later, to Miss Charlesworth.

'You know I'm really terribly glad about you and Bertie. It's really wonderful that she's at last got somebody she feels she can trust. You'll be a great help to her, I know.'

For the life of me I couldn't imagine how I could be of help to a lady like Miss Charlesworth, and to be perfectly honest I wasn't very interested.

'She's really got nobody in the world except me,' he said. 'And now you come along. Somebody she can really trust. A godsend.'

At this point I did what I thought was a clever thing. I decided to tease him a bit.

'I think,' I said, 'you're trying to flatter me.'

Lying flat on my back I looked up through the masses of gold-green branches, biting my lip, then laughing.

'Nothing farther from my mind.'

'Flatterer, that's what you are.'

'Don't girls like to be flattered?'

'Oh! to a certain extent I suppose,' I said in that airy, part mocking sort of way that adolescence deludes itself sounds like the tried wisdom of experience. 'All depends.'

Naturally he asked on what?

'I suppose,' I said, 'on she who is to be flattered.'

That was a fine self-revelatory remark if you like: not that I knew it at the time.

'Absolutely right,' he said. 'How clever of you.'

I laughed. Quite naturally it was clever of me.

Suddenly he turned his body, half sat up and leaned on one elbow, looking at me.

'May I ask you something?'

'Ask away,' I said. That cool thrill had started to creep up through my body again. 'I like answering questions.'

'Answer this then,' he said. His eyes were shining with excruciating brightness, even in the shade. 'If I say I like you without your hat, is that flattery?'

'No,' I said, laughing. 'That's a lie. Because you said you liked me with it.'

'It's neither,' he said. 'Because I love you with it and I love you without it. Either way.'

A moment later he was kissing me. He had an especially warm, obliterating way of kissing and though I suppose he must have kissed me in that same way hundreds of times afterwards I think I never quite got over that first fine careless bit of rapture. It was like being kissed, I remember thinking, by a man with all summer on his lips.

It might have been an hour or even two hours later that I roused myself from a half-dream and heard him talking yet again of Miss Charlesworth. By this time the top of my dress was all unbuttoned and I might have been lying on cushions of velvet as I lay there drowsily and listened.

'I really can't get over the fact that Bertie trusts you,' he was saying. 'Mind if I ask you something else?'

26

'Again? You and your questions.'

'Do you trust me?'

Involuntarily I lifted my hands and caught his face.

'Oh! of course,' I said. 'Of course I do. Absolutely. Always. Whatever made you think I mightn't?'

'Nothing. I just wanted to know.'

'Oh! that really hurt,' I said. 'I can't bear to feel that you even thought I didn't trust you.'

I started to look with prolonged earnest tenderness straight into his eyes, but before I could speak again the phantom figure of my mother was on the scene.

'I always trust people,' I said. 'Everybody. If you trust them they trust you. Don't you see?'

Except for that enchanting laugh of his Captain Blaine didn't bother to answer. A moment later he was forcing me gently back into the deep dry bed of leaves, stroking my hair and neck and discovering, for the first but not the last time, that mole on my naked shoulder.

4

I don't know if you've ever had the experience of hearing your soul singing on a dark night full of stars? Yes, I know it sounds ridiculous: too extravagantly silly for words. But that, in fact, is the way your soul is apt to behave on a dark night full of stars when you are only eighteen and a girl at that.

My soul did an awful lot of singing in July, August, and September of that year and not only on dark nights full of stars. It sang with equal rapture on white afternoons along the cliffs, through diamond dancing mornings by the sea and through breathless evenings in the forest or the car. First love, they will tell you, is apt to be a painful process, a complex fusion of heartache and joy, but I can only say that for me, during those three hot months, it was quite truthfully all joy, all singing.

Much of the joy arose, also, from the simplest things. Take, for example, our habit of lying on the cliffs and watching the sea. You might think that a man of forty and a good deal of experience, like Captain Blaine, would pretty soon grow tired of that.

Not at all. On the contrary it was he who would suggest, over and over again, that that was the way we should while away an evening or an afternoon. He had rather a pretty and amusing phrase for it, too.

He called it 'spying on our dream'.

I must explain all this with care. It's really of the utmost importance to convey exactly how that dream was conjured.

From the cliffs you can, of course, see miles out to sea. Ships from all over the world are passing and crossing all day and all night and on fine days you can see the cliffs of France with ease. By day they look like a piece of roughly cut cheese lying on the far horizon. By night you can pick out scores of lights from ships and lightships and shore.

It was those lights and those cliffs that formed the gateway to this dream of ours and it was Captain Blaine, lying on his back with those intensely iridescent eyes of his fixed on the sky, perhaps with his head in my lap, who was never tired of explaining it all to me. And naturally it was I, in turn, who was never tired of listening.

'Lovely spring days in Monte. And then over into Italy – Bordighera, San Remo, Lerici. The coast of flowers. Oh! Millions of flowers. Acres of carnations. Endless carnations even in winter. Lemon trees. Roses. Mimosa – it's the scent of mimosa that gets me. I never smell it without feeling I'm back there. Magical, extraordinary, how it takes you back. And there's a little restaurant down the street from the casino where they serve incredible prawns and you have iced Montrachet that's absolute nectar straight from heaven – what's that line? – "as though on manna I had fed and drunk the milk of paradise".'

Oh! yes, I forgot: Captain Blaine knew a little poetry too.

And it was always some remark of mine like 'Oh! darling I can't wait to get there' that set him laughing in that chuckling way of his and finally brought the conversation round to what he called the wherewithal.

'The pennies, girl, the pennies. There's the rub. Of course I'll get something when Bertie's snuffed it – but when, I ask you, when? Dammit, it's mine by right. I'm her only kith and kin. The sole remaining Blaine. You'd think she might cough up a little allowance for her only nephew, wouldn't you? But not Bertie. Oh! I love her, I adore the old girl, but I must say I get to thinking it's rather hard cheese sometimes.'

It was true, as my mother said, that he talked too much: but oh! how persuasively.

'I think she's mean,' I would say. 'Downright mean.'

'Oh, no, girl. Oh! no. Not mean. You've got her wrong there. Just careful, that's all. Just plain distrustful. That's what makes her go about in this snail-like fashion – carrying all her riches on her back. But when you think that just one bit of jewellery – and by the way she never wears the important bits, never – would fetch a comfortable fifteen hundred or perhaps even more I must say it tries the old faith a bit hard.'

'Selfish old thing.'

'That bedroom of hers must be just like a vault. An absolute treasure house. You won't believe this, I suppose, will you, girl? But when she lived down in the west country she had the place guarded by six wretched great mastiffs. One at the front gate, one at the back, one at the front door, one at the kitchen, one outside the bedroom door and one actually on the ruddy bed. Fortunately her doctor got wind of it and told her he strongly disapproved. Bad for the asthma and all that.'

'Is she likely to last long with this asthma?'

'Nature's wonderful, girl. Bertie's just a creaking gate. The sort that last for ever. No: I'm afraid there's nothing for it but to face things with the same fortitude and resignation the

Blaines have allegedly been famous for ever since Colonel James August Blaine amputated his own left leg at Blenheim with nothing but a potato peeler and a quart of brandy.'

Stupid though this no doubt sounds it was heaven to me to hear him talk like that. He really made you think that all that business of not being able to get his hands on Miss Charlesworth's money was nothing but mere lighthearted nonsense after all.

But for me it wasn't a lighthearted joke. More and more, as the summer went on, I found myself looking at the whole thing in that familiar trusting way of mine. I began again that old habit, so firmly instilled into me by my mother, of putting myself into other people's places, into and under other people's skins – in this case, Captain Blaine's.

I even began to talk about it. Not to my mother, naturally. My mother stood remarkably aloof from me in the matter of Captain Blaine. She stood apart like a silent shadow of disapproval – hoping, I suppose, that in the fullness of time I should get over it, as young girls are eternally supposed to get over their first fiery infatuations.

I began to talk, instead, to Ruby. Nothing pleased Ruby more than to talk to me of her newest loves – I really think she attached herself to a new uniform of some sort every time she went down to that beery Babylon of ours – and I must say she made a good listener when I talked to her of mine.

Finally, after one especially ecstatic confessional in her bedroom she said in a casual way that she hoped I hadn't done anything in any way naughty with Captain Blaine?

I wasn't slow to confess that I had in fact been naughty with Captain Blaine, not once but several times, and that I liked it. In fact, though I didn't say so, I was rather proud.

'Hope your mother don't get wind of it,' Ruby said. 'She wouldn't care much for that.'

'Oh! pot to mother.'

'Well, it's too late now, duckie,' Ruby said, 'but take my advice. Be careful.'

I laughed and said she was the one to talk, wasn't she?

'Oh! me, I'm different,' Ruby said. 'You can't count me. I'm past praying for, duckie. I like company, I do, and how many glasses o' stout do you think I can afford out o' the fifteen bob your ma pays me here? A girl's got to have a wet now and then, hasn't she? And if a chap pays for a few he's entitled to a bit of comfort, don't you think?'

After this Ruby gave one of her slow ripe laughs and said that you couldn't expect a man to give something for nothing all the time.

This sounded a good opportunity of saying that, as it happened, Captain Blaine had nothing to give.

'Don't get you, duckie.'

I went on to explain how broke Captain Blaine was and what a mean business it was he wasn't being helped by Miss Charlesworth.

'Officers are always broke, duckie. Live above their income by nature. It's the done thing. Take no notice o' that. Does he drink?'

'Not that I know of.'

'All officers drink, duckie. What about gambling? Cards?'

'I never heard him talk of it.'

'They all gamble, duckie. Second nature.'

I felt a little annoyed with Ruby for not understanding the situation more intelligently and I asked her rather tartly how she would like it if all her family fortune were tied up with one person while other people had to scrape along?

'Don't know about that, duckie, I'm sure. My ma left three pound ten to get herself buried with and fifteen bob still on the slate at the Queen's Head. That's all I know about fortunes.'

'Well, Miss Charlesworth's worth a fortune,' I said, 'and it's plain mean. Plain unfair. Some of her bits of jewellery alone are worth a thousand apiece.'

'Oh?' Ruby said. 'How did you find that out? Ever seen 'em?'

'Of course not,' I said. 'Captain Blaine told me.'

'I see,' Ruby said. 'I see.'

After that, in her casual, free and easy way, looking at me with those too-old, half-dissolute eyes of hers, Ruby used to ask me a great deal about Captain Blaine. But the curious thing was that though I talked on and on about him in that ecstatic confessional way of mine, telling her everything or practically everything, she didn't comment very much, though I didn't notice it very greatly at the time.

All I did notice was that she seemed consistently cool about all the stupendous ardours of my great affair, so much so that I went as far as to tell her one afternoon that I didn't think she had the remotest idea of what love was all about.

'Shouldn't wonder, duckie. Shouldn't wonder.'

In support of my claim, if you can believe it, I even quoted poetry at her. She didn't know, I supposed, a wonderful poem that began *I wonder, by my troth, what thou and I did till we loved*? Whether she did or not, I told her, that was how lovers all through the ages had felt and it included me.

'That's how you feel all right, duckie,' Ruby said. 'Well, once anyway.'

A few evenings later I was walking to the town to post some letters when I came upon Ruby and a Sergeant of Marines unsteadily winding sea-wards under the street gas-lights. The sergeant, in Ruby's words, was sloshed. Ruby, who was trying to save him from falling down, wasn't a great deal better. And as I dropped the letters into the box I heard the sergeant being sick in the gutter and Ruby, for some godless reason, laughing aloud.

No, Ruby, I said to myself, you just don't know. You never will know. Oh! how could you know?

5

It is always very difficult, I suppose, to say exactly where and how an obsession begins. It is rather like trying to trace the origins of a cold. What started it? Where did you pick up the germ? When did the chill begin?

I find it hard to recall now a single word of Captain Blaine's that might be said to have started my obsession with the key of one of Miss Charlesworth's jewel boxes. In fact I am perfectly sure that he was careful never to utter one. It was really much simpler to take me along the cliffs and hold me in long paradisal embraces and tell me how beautiful I was and invite me, in those extraordinary hypnotic words of his, to spy on our dream.

I forgot to say, by the way, that I often went to Miss Charlesworth's room. Part of her expression of trust in me – I rather think she went further than that, I think she even liked me – was to send for me quite often and ask me to perform various little services. I posted letters, bought stamps, changed books at the local library – nothing very much really, except that it meant that, as the summer went on, I became more and more familiar with the territory of that room.

It was the untidiest room I have ever seen. It was like the crazy repository of an industriously hoarding jackdaw. It was an elegantly shabby ruin of unlocked cabin trunks, travelling-cases, Gladstone bags, straw dress cases, handbags, reticules, sunshades, and umbrellas. And of course jewel cases – altogether five of them.

Looking back now, I feel more than ever certain that it was an afternoon in late September that my obsession with those boxes really started. Miss Charlesworth had asked if I would catch the six o'clock post with her letters and at the same time bring back some stamps for her.

But when I got back with the stamps and took them up to

her room and knocked on the door there was a sudden agitated jackdaw screech in answer.

'Yes? Who is it? Who is it? Who is it there now?'

'It's me,' I said. 'I've brought the stamps. It's Christine.'

'Christine, you must wait. Just a minute. Just a minute. Wait there.'

There was a sound of heavy trunks being moved. I heard the clatter of an overturning water jug as something struck the washstand.

After several minutes and more noises the key turned in the lock and the door opened to a gap of eight or nine inches. An agitated Miss Charlesworth appeared in the gap and put out a hand and said she would take the stamps now.

It was quite clear that one of the cabin trunks was wedged up against the door and I wondered why.

'What is it, Miss Charlesworth?' I said. 'Is anything the matter? Is there anything I can do?'

'No, nothing, nothing. Just give me the stamps, that's all.'

As I handed the stamps through the gap in the door I said:

'Are you sure, Miss Charlesworth? You haven't been trying to move those heavy trunks, have you?'

'No, no. I've just lost something. Mislaid something, that's all.'

I suggested that perhaps I might help her find it, whatever it was, but she hesitated before answering. She started licking her lips and swallowing very hard.

'Well, possibly you could. Perhaps you could. Your eyes are younger than mine.'

Though my eyes might have been younger they certainly weren't any keener than Miss Charlesworth's and it was only when I went into the room and found myself in the centre of that shabbily elegant ruin that I realized why it was that even she couldn't find what she was looking for.

Where only one jackdaw had worked before, a whole

flock, it seemed to me, had now been madly at work in the bedroom. Chairs and tables and chests-of-drawers and trunks were piled against each other. The carpet was half-rolled back. The bed was askew across the fireplace. The mattress was propped up at one end with a brass coal-scuttle and over by the window there was even an open pale pink sunshade.

The cause of all this, it seemed to me, was rather trivial. Miss Charlesworth had lost a key.

'Oh! is that all?' I said. 'We'll soon find that once we get things straightened out a bit.'

'I've been looking for over an hour already,' she said. 'Ever since you've been gone. It simply isn't here.'

'When did you last have it?'

'This afternoon. Early this afternoon.'

'Then it must be here,' I said. 'What sort of key is it?'

'It's the key of one of the jewel boxes,' Miss Charlesworth said. 'This one. The tortoiseshell.'

It was really very handsome, that big tortoiseshell box, with its silver lock and hinges. There was something very rich about the opulent polish of that deep brown shell. Involuntarily I smoothed my fingers across the lid of it and at the same moment I started thinking of Captain Blaine.

'Did you want something out of the box?' I said. 'Haven't you got another key?'

'I never have duplicate keys,' Miss Charlesworth said. 'I would never entertain the idea.'

'But if you had another key,' I said, 'you could open the box. It's all so simple.'

'I don't want to open the box!' she half-shouted at me. 'I don't want to open the box! I simply want to be sure that no one else has the key. All I want is the key.'

Obsessions, I suppose, often have the effect of clouding the faculties, upsetting the reason and that sort of thing. They are a kind of disease. In my case the effect was entirely opposite. In my first moment of obsession, confronted by a stupidly, agitated old woman fussing over a lost key, I began to feel remarkably logical, extraordinarily cool.

'Then we shall just have to set about finding the key,' I said, 'shan't we?'

It took me the better part of another hour to put some order into that crazy jackdaw chaos and at the end of it Miss Charlesworth was crying gently.

'It just simply isn't here. It just simply isn't here.'

The worst of over-heavy make-up is that it doesn't take very kindly to tears. Miss Charlesworth's face now looked like a rosy-mauve daub in a child's painting book when the colours have run.

'Please don't agitate yourself, Miss Charlesworth,' I said. 'It's all very simple. You must simply get somebody in the town to cut you another key.'

'Oh! no, oh! no, oh! no.'

In my cool way I took no notice of these protestations.

'In fact if I were you,' I said, 'I should have duplicate keys cut for all your cases at the same time. It's the only sensible, prudent thing to do.'

I think it was that word prudent that got her. She seemed to pull herself momentarily and sharply out of her agitation.

'Prudent? You mean to say you don't think I've been very prudent about matters?'

'No,' I said, 'frankly I don't. If you've got a box of jewellery and you can't open it what on earth's the use of it? It might just as well be full of sea-shells. In fact the really prudent thing would be to deposit the whole lot with a bank and forget it.'

'Oh! no. I hate banks. I distrust banks. I really distrust them.'

At this moment I took her by the hands. They were very skinny hands and they were hot and trembling.

'But you did say once you trusted me, didn't you, Miss Charlesworth?'

'Yes, I did. I did indeed.'

With cool reassurance I patted her hands.

'All right,' I said, 'I'll go down to Carter's the ironmongers in the morning and they'll send a man up.'

By this time she was crying again, though more vigorously than before, rather as if in relief, and at the same time saying between her sobs how greatly indebted she was to me for all my help and comfort and patience and so on. It really seemed an awful fuss to make over that stupid little key.

The following morning I got the man from Carter's to call. Before I left for the town Miss Charlesworth confided in me that she'd hardly slept a wink all night but that things were better now. She had seen the force of my logic suggesting that all four boxes should have new keys. It would be the prudent thing to do.

That, of course, is another curious thing about obsession. It breeds its own logic; everything about it has a way of seeming inevitable, of being right.

That was why, later on that afternoon, when I called at Carter's a second time and told them that Miss Charlesworth had changed her mind and had decided to have duplicate keys cut for all the boxes it seemed a logical rather than merely a clever part of the pattern.

Even Carter's agreed that it was the sensible, prudent thing to do.

6

It took about a week to get the keys made but, like the Frenchman who is warned that alcohol kills slowly, I was in no hurry. The holiday season in a seaside town is inevitably a great time for key-cutting. Hotel guests have a tiresome habit of losing keys or taking them away and forgetting to post them back.

I spent a good deal of that time trying to decide whether or not to tell Captain Blaine. It is of course not obsession that clouds the faculties or bends the reason at all, but pure innocence. And no one in the world could have been more obligingly, sublimely innocent than I was that summer. I have already described how my soul had acquired the habit of singing but you might well think that in three months it would have got over that. Not at all. Even seduction hadn't sullied me.

The rest of the time I spent in going over and over the fabric of my – or rather our – dream. I suppose it's really the oldest and most universal of all the silly dreams that women feed on: the desire to escape familiar drudgery, to exchange the commonplace for the celestial, to put trust in unfamiliar princes and finally be carried splendidly away.

In the same way I saw myself over and over again on the afternoon cross-channel steamer, eating dinner on the Blue Train, waking up to the carnation world of the Mediterranean, opening windows on to the blue heaven of Shelley's Italy. I was about to leave our rather stuffy little boarding house, the smell of frying fish and bacon, the front drawing-room that still actually had curtains of green chenille, antimacassars, and brass pots of aspidistra. I was going to leave the world of guests who didn't know how to behave at table, who complained of how the soup was cold and the potatoes underdone and bony, who fussed over damp sheets and forgot to tip the maids.

I was going, above all, to leave my mother, with her tedious philosophy of putting herself into other people's places, her infinite timidity and her spurious wisdom about trusting other people in order that they, in turn, could trust you. Weeks of silent disapprobation had turned my mother more and more into a kind of shadowy smudge and I was, thank God, going to escape from that too.

The day I collected the keys from the ironmongers I decided to tell Captain Blaine what I was doing – or rather to tell him half of it and later surprise him with the rest.

'Supposing I told you, darling, that I could get the money to go away,' I said. 'When could we go? Soon?'

'Now steady, girl,' he said. 'I'm a soldier. I just can't walk out like that.'

'You could get leave.'

'I suppose so. But where's this money coming from, girl? Dammit, I'm broke. I tell you I'm solid, stony broke.'

'You won't be tomorrow.'

'She talks to me in riddles,' he said. He laughed, half-mockingly I thought. 'She fills my head with dreams. But the cash, girl, the cash. Show me the tree where grows the cash.'

I loved, as I say, to hear him talk in that extravagant fashion and I said:

'Well, first I've got forty pounds of my own. We could buy the tickets with that.'

'With you now?'

Yes, I told him, I'd got it with me now. That made him laugh again, not mockingly this time, and he said:

'Comic, funny little girl. How long do you suppose we'd last on forty pounds?'

'Forty pounds is only the beginning,' I said. 'Tomorrow you can have a thousand.'

He gave a long sharp whistle of astonishment.

'There must be something wrong with your little head, girl,' he said. 'You must have got in a draught.'

No, I told him, there was nothing wrong with my little head and I hadn't been in a draught and there and then I decided to tell him the rest. When he heard what I had to say he suddenly took my face in his two hands in a rhapsodic gesture of delight.

'Clever little girl,' he said. 'I always knew you were a clever little girl.'

He couldn't have put it more plainly if he'd said outright that I'd done exactly what he hoped and expected I'd do. And in turn I felt supremely flattered because I'd so successfully put myself in his place, into and under his skin.

'Now this, I think,' he said, 'is what we'll do. Tomorrow, when I take Bertie for her drive, I'll invite the old girl out to lunch up in town. I'll lunch her at the Carlton. Oysters, champagne, pheasant, a marvellous soufflée, green Chartreuse. I

39

know she wants to see her lawyers in town and I'll say "Bertie dear, it's exhausting doing that journey back at the end of the day. I'll wire for a room for you for a couple of days. The change will pep you up. You were coughing yesterday".'

'And what then?'

He laughed: again, as I fondly understood it, not mockingly.

'The rest, dear girl,' he said, 'is largely up to you. What you have to look for is an emerald and diamond tiara. It's really big. You can't mistake it. No: perhaps not, after all. Too big. A bit too conspicuous. Better concentrate on rings. Bring a sample half dozen. They're mostly emerald and diamond too. That way we can dispose of them one at a time, whenever the champagne runs dry.'

Yes: he talked too much. But I, as I listened to him in brittle excitement, all tension, hardly talked at all. And later that night, in bed, I was vaguely aware that that brittle tension had been responsible already for a great change in me.

My soul had actually, at last, stopped its starry singing.

7

Two days later Miss Charlesworth went to London with Captain Blaine, who had my forty pounds in his pocket and a large companionable smile on his face as he called and drove her to the station. I still felt tense and brittle as I watched them from an upstairs window and I hardly knew how I'd get through the day until seven o'clock, when he'd be coming back again.

That afternoon was Ruby's half day. She generally left the boarding house about three o'clock but that day I decided to give her until four. But to my utter astonishment I was on my way up the back stairs, with a skeleton house-key to Miss Charlesworth's room in my hand, when Ruby suddenly came tripping down, humming happily to herself, all her war-paint on.

'Hello, duckie. Just off. Bit late today. Wrecked my face first time and had to do it all over again. Bit excited I expect.'

'Excited?'

I was so excited and staggered myself that I hadn't the wit to hide the key. I just stood there twisting it round and round in my fingers.

'Like the hat?' Ruby said. It was a big and floppy yellow straw, with a single magenta rose on it twice as large as a saucer. 'Had it re-trimmed. Excited? – I should say. It's my birthday. Going to lash out tonight and have supper at the Royal Clarence with my sister. You know, the one who works in the café. Been saving up for it. Going to do it big.'

Ruby gave one of her ripe explosive laughs and I, having nothing to say, simply stood there twisting the key.

'You look a bit pale, duckie,' Ruby said when that laugh of hers had finally stopped rudely slitting the air. She peered at me sharply from a face as heavily pink with powder as a marshmallow. She was really very handsome with all her war-paint on and you hardly knew her as the rather blowsy rag doll who, in the mornings, emptied bedroom slops and scrubbed the floors. 'Feeling under par?'

No, I was not, I told her and again I stood witlessly fumbling with the key.

'Well, cheery-bye, then,' Ruby said. My heart was racing frenziedly. 'Expect I'll be late. Going on to the Tennis Club dance afterwards. They'll probably wheel me home about four. Don't tell your Ma.'

I vaguely muttered something about wishing her a good time and then she was away downstairs. At the foot she turned and looked back at me, the heavy dark mascara on the lashes of her eyes making them look bigger and juicier than ever.

'Have a lay down, duckie,' she said. 'Don't like that look you got.'

A moment later the big floppy hat and the equally floppy dress, a bright petunia satin, had disappeared.

I gave her another five minutes and then let myself into Miss Charlesworth's bedroom. If my soul had stopped singing my heart certainly hadn't stopped racing and as I put the key into the tortoiseshell jewel box it felt like a toy windmill whirling madly round and round.

In my witless excitement I hadn't even had the sense to take the key out of the bedroom door and about a minute later the door suddenly opened and there stood Ruby.

There was a curiously impassive look on her juicy red lips and in those old grey eyes that I'd never seen before and she simply stood for a full minute without speaking, quietly staring through me.

When she spoke at last it was in a level whisper. It couldn't have startled me more if it had been a bomb.

'Looking for something, duckie?'

I couldn't speak. My tongue felt frozen. I simply stood there goggling. And then something extraordinary happened. At the very moment when I felt sure she was about to start pleading with me about this and that she simply uttered one more sentence and it hit me like a whip.

'I'll drink your health tonight, duckie,' she said, again in that level whisper, 'I really will.'

That was all. I actually felt my eye-balls jump and a moment later that big floppy hat of hers had disappeared completely for the second time.

I suppose I stood there for fully half a minute before realizing that the only clever thing to do was to try and call her back. I remember actually rushing out on to the landing and calling 'Ruby' several times before realizing with horror that some-one else might hear me. It was too late anyway by that time and all I could think of doing next was to rush back into the bedroom, grab up seven or eight rings and then lock the box and the bedroom door before scrambling upstairs to my room.

For the next three hours I couldn't make up my mind who I wanted to see most: Captain Blaine or Ruby. I lay on the bed in unparalleled idiotic confusion, incapable of thinking, my mind a jelly. I hadn't even looked to see what the rings were like but had simply thrown them loose, like so many peppermint lumps, into my bag.

At seven o'clock I went out to meet Captain Blaine. At the eastern end of the front there used to be public gardens with lawns and beds of geraniums and fuchsia in summer-time and it was a good place for meeting. I waited there till eight o'clock. I've explained before, I think, how Captain Blaine often kept me waiting, sometimes for an hour or more. 'Not because I didn't want to come, girl, but because other chaps decreed otherwise,' was how he would charmingly explain it. 'In the army most of the money and the time you have are really some-one else's.'

At half past eight I walked to the railway station. There were two more trains from London that night: one at nine and the last at midnight. When Captain Blaine didn't come on the nine o'clock train I walked up the hill to the garrison. Now and then I saw an officer or a group of officers walking towards me down the hill and my heart started racing again. But Captain Blaine was never among them and by ten o'clock I was back in the gardens, staring at the flowers.

I went over the same futile procedure a second time after meeting the train at midnight and it was one o'clock in the morning before I was back outside the rear door of the boarding-house, waiting for Ruby. It was getting cold by that time and now and then I had an intolerable fit of trembling.

Yet the most vivid thing I can remember about that grotesque wandering of mine is not the cold or the trembling or the impossible racing of my heart every time I heard footsteps in the darkness, but the curious sensation that I had no longer any legs. I had somehow been left with two fleshless husks, above which my body simply drifted emptily along.

It was after three o'clock when Ruby finally appeared. I knew it was Ruby some time before she got to me. It was not

43

merely that I recognized that big floppy straw hat and its magenta rose as she swung it under the one remaining street light.

Ruby, unlike me, was in a happy frame of mind. She was singing.

8

'Hullo, duckie,' she said and it was almost as if she knew I'd be waiting there. 'You'll miss your beauty sleep if you're not careful, won't you?'

Without hesitation she threw back her blonde head and laughed in that rich, air-splitting fashion of hers. Then she swung unsteadily on her feet and did a complete turn on her heels, ending up with her back to me.

'Do me up, duckie, will you?' she said. 'I've come unput somehow. I'm blowed if it didn't feel a draught down my back and now I know.'

I didn't speak a word. My hands were cold too and they trembled as I did up four or five buttons at the back of her dress. I couldn't do up the two top buttons because they were missing and in fact the dress was torn for five or six inches at one side of the neck, as if someone had tried to rip it off her.

'Torn a bit, aren't I?' she said. 'Thought so. Comes of struggling.' She laughed in rousing fashion again. She wasn't quite sloshed. She was just gay and happy. 'Never struggle, duckie. Don't know, though. It's more fun. They like it better if you do.'

All this time we were about a hundred yards from the boarding house and we hadn't moved an inch nearer since meeting. I didn't want to move either until I'd asked her one question.

'Ruby,' I said. 'I want to ask you something. Are you going to tell anyone you saw me in Miss Charlesworth's bedroom?'

'Me?' Ruby said. She swayed tipsily on her heels, at the same time swinging the big straw hat. 'Duckie, I never tell tales out of school.'

In my distraught and stupid innocence I actually wanted to thank her but before I could find the words she said:

'Drank your health, duckie. Like I said I would. And guess who with?'

The sergeant of marines struck me as the most likely companion for our Ruby at health-drinking time, but the thought of him had hardly crossed my mind before she was laughing again and saying:

'Your friend. You know. Your friend.'

'What friend?'

'Your captain. Miss Charlesworth's nephew. Him.'

The strange sensation of having no legs extended itself suddenly to the rest of my body. I remembered simply floating there like an empty husk, speechless, frozen stiff.

'Me and my sister saw him first at the Royal Clarence. Supper with champagne and oysters. With a friend of his, Lieutenant Pascoe. Know him? Thin fellow, very dark, with a moustache. Started making eyes at my sister while we were eating our peach melba. She's a corker, my sister. She's the pretty one.'

I was still speechless, just a husk.

'Then this Lieutenant Pascoe sends the waiter over and says would we have a glass of the widow? They were celebrating some battle or other. Can't think of the name now. Couldn't understand what he meant by the widow at first and then it turns out it's champagne. Are you listening, duckie?'

I was listening; but not with my ears. That wretched, idiotic soul of mine was the only thing about me capable of that simple act of reception.

'Well, I could see this Lieutenant was plain sunk on my sister. Couldn't blame him, either, could you? She's the glamour kid. Figure like an hour glass. Hardly any waist.

45

Long legs and a bust like Venus. She's a lot younger than me too and she's got the look in her eye.'

As she was saying all this she swung the hat again and did a few staggering whirls on the pavement, half in the act of dancing.

'Then before you know what's happening we're all in Captain Blaine's car and off to the Tennis Dance, with my sister practically on the lieutenant's lap at the back and me in front with the captain. Am I telling the tale all right, duckie?'

She was telling the tale all right. How much of it was gospel truth I was too distraught to decide, but I've since often comforted myself with the thought that I suppose you really need to have lost innocence, as Ruby had, before you really understand it.

'Then the fun started. My sister's the one that always causes it. She lets the men dance close to her and it drives them up the cliff. She does it on purpose. She says so. It makes 'em mad. By the way, I thought you said the Captain didn't drink?'

Ruby laughed again in what I then thought was a horribly raw, distasteful way.

'Not much, duckie, not much. One of these days they'll float a cross-channel boat on what he puts away. I'll say this though. He never gets mardy and moody on it. He knows what to do with a girl.'

Have you ever seen anyone shocked into speechlessness? Two or three years ago I saw a young man on a cross-channel steamer, in a rough passage, who was shocked by fright into a temporary dumb paralysis. The stewards had to hold him up. Like mine, his legs might just as well not have been there and his lips and his tongue were incapable of working.

I was paralysed too as I stood there staring at Ruby. Even my wretched soul wasn't doing much listening by that time. And what, after all, can you expect? How much can you ask of your soul? After weeks of abandoned singing you can't suddenly start asking it to play at mathematics and work out emotional logarithms, can you? You simply can't ask it that.

46

I haven't the remotest idea of how much longer Ruby and I stood there on the pavement together but suddenly that raw laugh of hers was splitting the air again and she was saying:

'Oh! he knows what a girl wants all right. Not surprised you let him do what he likes with you. Who wouldn't? He can give you the lot and well wrapped up too. Needn't have ripped my dress though. I was all ready to take it off in the car if he'd waited.'

Suddenly everything inside me broke. The use in my legs came back with such a stunning shock that I started running. I could really hear again. I caught on the night air the noise of a gull croaking across the harbour, then the sound of my own feet and then the last raw peal of Ruby laughing.

A few minutes later I was dashing up the back stairs of the boarding house when suddenly I heard my mother hissing at me. I had utterly forgotten my mother and now it was she who shocked me to a standstill.

'Where ever have you been, child? Where on earth have you been? My dear God, where ever have you been?'

I hadn't time to answer this agitated heart-cry before Ruby was there behind her at the foot of the stairs, casually swinging the big yellow straw hat and saying in the sweetest, friendliest, most off-hand way, as if we'd just got back from a picnic:

'Been to the Tennis Dance with me, ma'am. I'm to blame. Should have ought to have told you. It's all right, ma'am. It's done her the world of good to have a bit of dancing.'

9

My mother is dead now. Ruby is dead too. She was having a drink with a Polish sailor one evening in the Prince of Orange, in the middle of the blitz, when a thousand-pounder blew both of them, and the pub, to all eternity. The boarding-house got its own hit a little later and I live now with my husband in a flat at the other end of the promenade. Oh! yes, I'm married, and most respectably.

I still like to walk by the sea. I'm still fond of taking my thoughts for solitary airings along the shore. And sometimes on fine hot summer days I find myself looking at the yellow chimney pots that are so like organ pipes and the gulls that sit on them so like fat blue owls.

And sometimes when I look up at them the brilliance of the light tricks me again. I'm temporarily blinded and the sky is empty. All I am aware of is the raw hungry croak of gulls, which in turn remind me of the voice of Ruby, talking to me in the days when my soul did such a lot of singing.

'Yes, that's how you feel all right, duckie. Well once, anyway.'

And then the trick of light is over. From the far parapets of the castle and the high white cliffs of chalk down to the smallest glistening crests of the sheltered waves in the harbour and the blue plump feathers of the screeching gulls sitting on those impossible yellow chimney pots every detail shows up with unmistakable reality.

For the space of a second or two I can smell once again the breath of corruption. Then I give a long cold shudder of relief and it's all as clear as crystal in the summer air.

A Month by the Lake

OVER the lake the weather had settled into such tranquil late magnificence that Miss Bentley had decided to stay another month: the entire month of October.

Already in the distances the morning mountains sometimes revealed the thinnest night-caps of pure fresh snow; but below them, by noon, every fissure in the bare perpendicular falls of rock was distinctly carved, clear dark purple in the sun. Even farther below them the masses of pine and chestnut and beech and walnut caught the smouldering light of afternoon like clusters of solid coral, pale amber, bronze or bright rusty from the harsh heat of summer. Still farther below them the vines on their narrow terraces were hung with palest ripe green grapes, misted with olive bloom. Farthest below of all, below the umbrella pines, the erect black plumes of cypresses and the shining flowerless thickets of camellia, tender torches of oleanders still bloomed along the lakeside: pure white, pale yellow, pink and vermilion, flowering in front of houses that melted into the honied impermanence of soft distances until they were nothing but stumps of burned-down candles melting in pearly air.

One by one Miss Bentley had watched the guests of the white *albergo* depart until now, at last, only herself and Major Wilshaw remained. By noon, now, Major Wilshaw too would be gone: a ghost departed with the family of machine-tool manufacturers from Milan, charmers all, the husband a joker in cool sky-blue suits, the wife a splendid cushion of dark fat velvet, the two little girls like sallow angels for whom Major

Wilshaw was fond of doing tricks with handkerchiefs, English pennies and bits of string.

With them had gone the two American ladies, school-teachers from Ohio, who had become ill, as Miss Bentley had firmly predicted they would, from living too much on ice-water, green salad and uncooked pears. And with them all the rest whose time or money or interest was not unlimited: the Swiss honeymooners from Schaffhausen, the German chemist and his wife from Frankfurt, the two couples from Yorkshire whom Miss Bentley had christened the gawpy-talkies, the car dealer and his alleged wife, really mistress, from Brussels – mistress, Miss Bentley was sure, because she always passed him the sugar at breakfast, although he clearly never took sugar in his coffee – and finally the sock-knitting English governess with the silent, fallow-timid boy from Turin, a little wooden human carving snatched from the shadows of some impossible Catholic altar.

Now, when Major Wilshaw had gone, there would be no one left but herself; Maria, who cleaned the bedrooms; Enrico, who waited at table; the two cooks and Signora Fascioli, who owned the hotel.

Alone, she would watch the lamps of summer burn quickly out; she would eat another ton of spaghetti – Bolognese or Milanese on alternate days, except Sundays, when it was tagliatelli – peel with meticulous care the last of the pears and purple figs, manicure her nails every Wednesday and Saturday, wash her hair every Friday, swim when she felt like it and take at least one more excursion by funicular to the Monte and look down for the last time on the lake below – its great pattern of inlets and curves, she always thought, so like some great blue glass lioness, sprawled and glittering between the mountains and the plain.

From her favourite place on the patio, a viewpoint from which she could watch the lake-steamers glide like long white water-birds from the gap between the two islands opposite the hotel, Miss Bentley watched Major Wilshaw come down the hotel steps, folding up, with care, the bill he had just paid.

'Ah! there you are. Thought I should find you here.'

The most remarkable feature of Major Wilshaw was not, in Miss Bentley's eyes, the singularly fine straight nose; or the way the greyish hair crinkled bushily into his neck, or the sharp pale blue eyes; or the fact that he had, with his loose brown trousers, bright blue shirt and chrome yellow tie, a rather gay, gamey appearance, an air of wishing to be something rather dashing.

To Miss Bentley the most remarkable feature about Major Wilshaw were his small flat pink ears. They were not only exceptionally small for a man who was thickish, upright and rather tall. They were very delicately, very intricately fashioned. Nothing in the entire human body, Miss Bentley would tell herself, had quite the same fascinating quality as ears. All the attraction of mood and response and character and emotion lay, of course, in the mouth and eyes: everyone knew that. But ears were, Miss Bentley thought, far more wonderful. Ears were unchanging and undying. They remained, in some strange way, uncoarsened, undepraved, unwrinkled and unaged by time. In the ears of the aged you could see the flesh of youth; in a sense they were immortal and never grew old.

Perhaps it was for this reason that Miss Bentley always greeted Major Wilshaw with oblique, off-the-target glances, never looking him straight in the eyes.

'Well: I'm afraid it's good-bye.'

'Oh! come, surely not good-bye,' Miss Bentley said. 'Say *arrivederci*.'

She smiled, putting her book on the little white wooden table at her side. At forty-seven she could give Major Wilshaw a few years, she thought, though perhaps not very many. His hair was already grey; her own was still a rich honey brown, without a touch of age.

'What time does your train go?' she said. 'I forget.'

The train, she knew quite well, went at half past twelve. She saw it regularly every day, creeping up from Milan along the lakeside.

'Half past twelve.'

'Really! I thought it was earlier.'

'No: half past,' the major said. 'Twelve thirty-one to be exact.'

Something, she suddenly thought, seemed to be troubling him. He took from his pocket his newly paid hotel bill and began to examine it covertly.

'So you're really going,' she said.

'I'm really going.'

'Which way are you going?' she said. 'You did tell me. I forget.'

She had not forgotten. She knew very well that he was going by way of Domodossola, the Simplon, Brig, Montreux, Lausanne and the spaces of France beyond.

'Via Domodossola, the Simplon, Brig, Montreux and that way,' he began to say and then broke off, looking perplexed. 'I don't think my bill's quite right,' he said, 'it doesn't somehow –'

A little fussily the major began to examine the bill, turning his head sideways towards her, so that once again she could see the fine, small ears. Miss Bentley thought there were many ears, even male ones, that were like sea-shells; but the fascination of Major Wilshaw's ears was much more like that of certain flowers. Perhaps that was ridiculous and which particular flower they most resembled was something that, so far, had persisted in eluding her; but she was perfectly sure that, one day, she would discover which one it was.

'No: it isn't right,' he said. 'They've charged me far too much –'

Folding and re-folding the bill, he looked up at her, helpless and troubled.

'May I look?' she said. 'Perhaps – '

'Please,' he said. 'Please. I always say it pays to check these things – '

Miss Bentley took the bill, read through it once and gave it back to him.

'It adds up all right to me,' she said. 'I think you're adding the one as a one instead of as a seven. See? – it has the little stroke across its middle.'

'Of course, of course, how stupid,' the major said.

Below, across the lake, the peep of a steamer whistle broke the tranquil morning air, echoed across the flat honey-blue water and re-echoed in the scarcely visible mountains.

'That's the twelve o'clock steamer,' Miss Bentley said.

'Already?' the major said. 'I'm afraid I must go if it is. I'm afraid it's good-bye.'

'Are you always nervous when you travel?' Miss Bentley said.

'Well, not exactly nervous. But you know – '

'Just in a state of this and that. I know,' she said. 'You feel you're neither here nor there.'

That, he had noticed, was a favourite phrase of hers: a state of this and that. She was rather given to such odd, half-slangy quips that hit off moments, people and moods with dry and sometimes satirical exactitude.

'That's it, that's it,' he said. 'A state of this and that. Wondering if you've got everything. If there's anything you've forgotten.'

'And have you got everything?'

'I think so, I fancy so.' Uncertainly he fumbled at the pocket of his jacket. 'I checked – '

'Ticket?'

'Yes, yes. Ticket.'

'Passport? You told me you once forgot your passport.'

'In my suitcase.'

'Never keep it in your suitcase,' she said. 'You're done if

53

someone snitches it. Suitcase and passport gone in one. Always keep it on you.'

'Of course, of course,' he said. 'I'll do it. I'll see to that.'

'Well then,' she said, 'if you've got everything.'

She got up and the major extended his hand.

'Well, good-bye, Miss Bentley. It's been absolutely –'

'Oh! not here,' she said. 'I'm coming down the steps.'

'How nice of you, how kind,' he said. 'There's absolutely no need –'

Miss Bentley was suddenly aware, as she descended the white steps of the terrace slightly behind him, of two eventful things. The first was the unexpected elucidation of the private mystery that had troubled her ever since the first evening she had seen the major doing tricks for the amusement of the two sallow little angels from Milan.

It was the sudden revelation that the major's left ear was, more than anything, like a small pink rose. The particular rose she had in mind was flattish, inclined to be oval in shape, and mysteriously crinkling to a soft inner heart.

'So it is,' she said and the major, turning to say 'Pardon?' saw on her face a look of extraordinary revelation.

'Did you say something?'

'No,' she said. 'No. Nothing at all.'

A moment later she was aware of the second event. Voices were suddenly laughing gaily in Italian by the front door of the hotel. Signor Fascioli was rushing down the steps, laughing too. And there, by the door of a cream familiar Fiat, were the two sallow little angels from Milan, dancing up and down yellow dresses flouncing. The splendid dark fat cushion of a wife was there and Signor Bompiani, gay and immaculate in light blue linen, was waving both hands above his head in the direction of Miss Bentley and Major Wilshaw, giving greeting in the manner of a boxer:

'Major! Miss Bentley! We are here! Back again! Time for a nice cup of tea!'

This was his favourite, much-repeated joke about the English.

'Not to *stay*?'

'To stay. Of course. The weather is so beautiful – *bella, bella, bella* – To stay, of course!'

'*Molto bella*,' Miss Bentley said. 'Oh! so beautiful. How nice to see you.'

'Shake hands, Major, shake hands.'

'The major is going,' Miss Bentley said. 'You're just in time to say good-bye.'

'The major is going? No? Where? Why? Away? Not –'

'Away,' the major said. 'England.'

'We arrive. You depart. That's very sad. That's not very well arranged, Major –'

The two sallow little angels began dancing about Major Wilshaw, pleading in Italian, pulling his sleeves and hands.

'They wish a trick!'

'Oh! no. I'm sorry. I must get the train –'

'They wish one trick before you go!'

'It's getting awfully late –'

'In the car they speak of nothing but tricks. Tricks from the major. They wish all the time tricks from the major!'

'Just one then. One quickly –'

The major, stooping down, began to do his little trick with English pennies. It consisted, in essentials, of losing the pennies one by one in the hair of – but suddenly, in surprise, Miss Bentley was not watching.

In the excitement she had not noticed, by the door of the car, a girl with smooth fair hair, wearing a plain black skirt, rather full, and a plain white blouse. Nor had the major seen her either; but now, suddenly, the trick completed, he straightened up, turned and caught sight of her standing there.

Miss Bentley had never seen in the eyes of a girl a look of such open unequivocal indifference, so cool in contemplation, and suddenly Signor Bompiani was saying:

'Ah! badly arranged again, forgive me, badly arranged. I am

55

so sorry – this is Miss Beaumont. She is with us for three months to learn Italian and also to teach the kids a little English, I hope. Miss Beaumont, please to allow me to introduce Miss Bentley and Major Wilshaw.'

'How do you do,' Miss Beaumont said.

On the major's face a stunned, excruciating look of pure shyness developed into one of actual embarrassment. Opening his mouth to speak he succeeded only in giving a brief gape of astonishment. At the same time he averted his face, as if unable suddenly to look at the girl.

'The taxi has been waiting ten minutes, Major Wilshaw,' Signora Fascioli said. 'You will miss the train – '

'Oh! must you go, Major?' Signor Bompiani said. 'No more tricks?'

'I must go, I must really get on. I'll say good-bye – '

'Good-bye then, Major. Good-bye,' Signor Bompiani said. 'You will miss the train, Major!'

'Good-bye! Good-bye!' the angels shouted.

'Not good-bye,' Miss Bentley said. '*Arrivederci*!'

'*Arrivederci*!' everyone shouted. '*Arrivederci*!'

'*Arrivederci*,' the major said. 'Good-bye.'

Framed against the exquisite background of the lake, the major lifted his hand and took off his small green homburg hat in farewell. Behind him the mountains, half-dissolved in dreamy amber haze, threw into sharp relief the yellow tie, the glazed blue eyes and above all the small pink ears for which Miss Bentley felt she had found, at last, the perfect, happy comparison.

She, too, raised her hand, waving it in farewell; and then realized, a moment later, that the eyes of the major were not looking back at her. Nor were they looking at Signora Fascioli, the Bompianis, Maria and Enrico, or the little angels who, no longer dancing, were simply crooking slow, sad fingers.

They were not even looking at Miss Beaumont. With melancholy transparence they appeared to be held in a trance by which it seemed almost certain for a second or two that the major had forgotten who and where he was. He stood for a moment longer in this lost enchantment, eyes blank and almost white in the sun, and then suddenly turned and groped into the taxi.

'Come back next year!' Miss Bentley called and down on the lake the short rude peep of the departing steamer mocked the flawless distances in answer.

Three-quarters of an hour later, sitting alone at her table under the arbour of virginia creeper at the end of the patio, Miss Bentley was raising a glass of *valpolicella* to her lips in readiness to wash down the last mouthful of *spaghetti bolognese*. The glass never reached her lips and as she set it slowly down on the table, with a surprise far greater than she had seen on the face of Major Wilshaw when he had first become aware of the cool detached Miss Beaumont, her mouth too fell open, as the major's had done, with a gape of astonishment.

The major himself was just driving up to the hotel in an open taxi, holding his green homburg hat on his knees.

Her first impulse, as the taxi drew up, was to call out to him. Then she checked it. A great air of preoccupation shrouded the major, who was staring down at his feet.

She turned quickly to glance at the Bompianis and Miss Beaumont, lunching at their long table at the farther end of the arbour. The two children were drinking red wine in water and Miss Beaumont, with white meticulous fingers, was washing, peeling and eating a bunch of pale green grapes. Miss Beaumont, she realized for the first time, was, in her thin, measured way, a very pretty creature.

When she looked back at the road through the screen of virginia creeper leaves she saw Maria was helping to unload the major's suitcases but that the major had already disappeared. Instinctively she looked up towards the window of the room he occupied on the second floor of the hotel and then realized how stupid it was to expect to see him there so quickly or even to see him there at all. At the same time she found herself suffering from the temporary illusion that the major had, after all, not appeared on the road from the lake so suddenly.

'It was probably,' she thought, 'that I just wanted him to appear.'

Three or four minutes later Enrico, the thin hollow-eyed waiter, came out of the hotel carrying tablecloth, napkins, cutlery, pepper and salt pots and a small white plate. She watched him lay the table that the major always occupied and then, when he had finished, called him over.

'Is there another visitor?'

'The table,' he said, 'is for Major Wilshaw.'

'The major left this morning for Domodossola.'

'The major is back.'

'Did he miss the train?'

'I think so, madam. I don't know.'

'Bring my fruit,' she said, 'will you please?'

For the next three quarters of an hour she sat washing and peeling the grapes and dark blue figs of which she never tired. She washed the fruit slowly and thoughtfully, watching with fascination the pearls of air gather delicately on the grapeskins under the water, her eyes at the same time ready to lift themselves towards the door of the hotel.

After twenty minutes the Bompianis got up from their table. Mrs Bompiani, who did not speak English, smiled in Miss Bentley's direction as she rose. Mr Bompiani, red-flushed beneath the eyes from wine, smiled at Miss Bentley too and said simply, with satisfied brevity: 'Shut-eye.' The two children waved spidery fingers and Miss Beaumont, who had changed her white blouse for a scarlet sleeveless one, seemed to begin to smile and then decided not to.

After the voices of the children had died away the afternoon became quite silent, wrapped in thin hot haze. The lake took on a golden glassy skin, without a stir of air. Once Enrico appeared at the door of the hotel, looked in Miss Bentley's direction, saw that she was still peeling grapes and then went away.

It was nearly an hour before she saw the major, who had changed now into a light shantung suit slightly creased from packing, with a brown silk shirt and pale green tie, walking towards her under the screen of virginia creeper.

'I suppose you're surprised?'

'Not a bit,' she said. 'I felt all along you'd mistaken the time of the train.'

'I didn't miss the train.'

He glanced round as if, she thought, looking for the Bompianis, and then said:

'May I join you? I'm not eating.'

'No lunch?'

'They're bringing me some coffee.'

She sat for some moments contemplating in silence the small pink ears. She thought there seemed something covert, complicated and sad about Major Wilshaw, more especially about the eyes, which were downcast as he played with a spoon, not often looking up at her.

'So you came back.'

'I came back.'

She decided suddenly, for no reason, not to ask why.

'You should have something to eat,' she said. 'You look tired.'

'Do I? I don't feel it,' he said. 'I'll be all right with just the coffee.'

Flawlessly the lake lay shining in the afternoon sun, the oleanders alight along the shore. She found herself not only extraordinarily glad that he was back but even happier not to be alone. Then when Enrico brought the coffee she found herself instinctively passing the sugar, saying:

'Sugar? You take a lot, I know.'

Thoughtfully unwrapping the sugar cubes, Major Wilshaw

stared with light blue eyes at the hazed quiet skin of the lake.

'What do you do when you suddenly have damn funny impulses?' he said.

She found herself laughing.

'Oh! I suppose you don't have such things,' he said.

'Why not? I have wild, unconquerable desires too,' Miss Bentley said, 'if it comes to that.'

She was sorry, a moment later, that she had mocked him. That was rather her way sometimes, she thought, to mock, to be a little trite. It was not really herself who spoke on such occasions. It was really – puzzled, she shied away from a complexity too difficult to explain.

'I'm talking about an impulse that stops you,' the major said. 'Not the other kind.'

'Not the urging, to-hell-with-it kind?'

'No. The sort with a voice,' he said.

This is too ridiculous, she thought. Men simply don't talk like this. Nor women either.

'No, seriously, seriously,' he said.

'You're going to tell me you were walking across the station, ready to get on the train, when a voice said, "Don't go. Don't do it. Go back to the *Albergo Bianco* and stay a few more days".'

'Something like that.'

'That was simply commonsense speaking. You needn't have gone in the first place. You know that. In this marvellous, wonderful weather.'

'I know it sounds silly – '

'Not a bit. Not silly at all. Commonsense. The sanest, most sensible thing to do. Who'd leave all this if they didn't have to? Look at it!' With rapturous hands she pointed down to the lake laced in its tender honey-skin of autumn light. 'Not me, that's certain. I'm not sure I shan't stay all winter.'

He started to speak, then stopped and poured himself more coffee. She pushed the sugar-bowl across to him a second time

60

and then watched him unwrap two of the papered cubes and drop them in the cup.

'You're walking along a street to go somewhere. You know perfectly well where you're going – what time and so on and all that. And suddenly you don't go. You're turned back by something and the whole day, perhaps a great bit of life, is different. You've done that surely?'

Of course she had done that, she told him. Everybody had done that.

'Do you feel life has a pattern?' he said. 'A predetermined one, I mean?'

'Oh! Heaven help us,' she said. 'Don't go into that. If I'd felt my life had had a predetermined pattern I'd probably have cut my throat at the age of six.'

She laughed again, but she noticed that he did not laugh in reply.

'How long are you going to stay?' she said, 'now you're back?'

He simply shrugged his shoulders slightly, an almost imperceptible muscular quiver, and again lifted his coffee cup.

'Stay a whole month,' she said. 'Stay until another impulse strikes you.'

He gave the faintest of smiles and then started biting his lip.

'Well, here we all are again,' she said, 'anyway. You, the Bompianis, those two little angels and me. I think it's absolutely wonderful.'

'Yes.'

'Do you remember that picnic we had in the mountains?' she said. 'Do you suppose we could manage another picnic like that? I'd cheerfully arrange it if the Bompianis would offer the car like they did last time. I'm sure they would, except that this time, of course, there's Miss Beaumont –'

'Oh?' He spoke very abruptly, almost sharply. 'Is that her name?'

'I think that's what they said –'

'I didn't catch it, I didn't catch it,' he said.

'I shall always remember that picnic. That cold spring water the children washed their feet in and the wild raspberries and the little wild cyclamen they were selling along the roadside, at the village down the valley. I'd never seen wild cyclamen before. I didn't even know there were wild cyclamen –'

She broke off and saw, from the far-away look on his face, that the major was not listening. Nor was he looking at her. And then she remembered, suddenly, when she had seen that same look of lost enchantment on his face before.

And getting up from the table, pushing away her glass and picking up her book, she remembered Miss Beaumont. It was Miss Beaumont who had inspired it all.

About four o'clock Major Wilshaw walked down to the town, called at the post office and sent a telegram to the Wilshaw Light Metal Construction Co. Ltd, of which he was managing director, saying 'Delayed for further week possibly more address me as previously case urgency.' Then he bought himself a day-old English newspaper from the kiosk at the steamer landing stage, glanced at the headlines and walked back to the hotel.

He had already changed his clothes a second time. Now he was wearing a soft blue suit in mohair with a deep cream shirt and a pale blue silk tie. His shoes were of light brown turned calf and he was without a hat. His grey hair was well and scrupulously brushed, giving him a certain military appearance, though in fact he was not a military man. During the war he had joined up in his age-group as his turn came and had risen to the rank of major in the Royal Engineers purely because he was an engineer by profession and because establishment happened to call for another major at a certain time. He never stopped to ask why, after the war, he continued to use his rank. A great many majors and quite a few captains did and he never stopped to ask why they did so either. During a war so many people got into the habit of using ranks and after the war it was natural and easy to go on with it as before.

At fifty-one he was unmarried, successful, prodigiously competent, and, as he liked to think, very young in mind. His impression of Miss Bentley was that she was, in spite of her ungreyed brown hair, her liveliness of speech and generally pleasant air, well settled in middle age. He thought that he could give her quite a few years. One of the things that success in business enabled him to do was to expend a good deal of time, care and money on his choice of clothes. He thought a man ought not only to dress well but, rather like an animal adopting protective colouring, to dress according to his immediate surroundings. That was why he wore simple plain blue suits at the office, sober clerical greys when he did business in London and now, on the lake, a variety of light, sunny blues, yellows, browns and greens that matched the burning autumn mountains, the honey expanses of water, the oleanders, the Italianate villas and skies. That, he thought, was the kind of thing that kept him young.

During the three weeks he had been on the lake he had become quite friendly, in an unadventurous detached sort of way, with Miss Bentley. She was what he called a decent old stick. She was not at all bad-looking, he thought, and she dressed herself rather as his secretary in the office did, neatly and freshly, with what he called a slightly starched-and-ironed effect. She used just enough make-up to keep herself from dullness. Her hands and hair were always scrupulous. He was unaware that she found the shape of his ears both baffling and attractive or that she had searched for a long time for a fitting description of their delicacy. She had a certain mustardy sense of humour, a little dry and hot on the tongue as it were, and when she trotted out phrases like 'Oh! I have wild and unconquerable desires if it comes to that' he knew she was merely being funny and that she didn't mean it at all. Or perhaps, he thought, it was a sort of protection against something, though what it was he didn't know.

63

What Miss Bentley called his rather gay and gamey air rose largely from his choice of clothes; but it sprang also from a conviction that he was attractive to girls. He rather fancied himself in that way. At home, in the town where the Wilshaw Light Metal Construction Company occupied several pleasant acres of ground, he ran about in an open cream sports car, played tennis, belonged to a country club and knew of one or two hotels in the country where the food was good. From time to time he struck up acquaintances with girls who also ran about with him in the sports car, played tennis, belonged to the country club, went to eat with him in country hotels and then, for some reason he could never define, suddenly left him to marry men who toiled in printing works, ran unsuccessful market gardens or were just plain ten-pound-a-week clerks in offices. He could never understand these things; it puzzled him always to wonder why.

At fifty-one his figure was still good, if a little solid, the stomach muscles still hard and taut, and one of the things he did rather well was to play tennis. On holidays he always took a couple of rackets with him, together with a supply of good correct clothes. But people generally, he thought, didn't play tennis quite so much as before and he found it always rather hard to get a partner.

Once he asked Miss Bentley if she played and all he had got was one of her mustardy answers:

'Oh! Love and all that. No. I'm afraid it never attracted me. Oh! except one thing – that business of love meaning nothing. Why does it? Of course one knows it does anyway, but did some cynic start the game?'

As he walked back along the road to the hotel he remembered his tennis. He remembered too his explanation of why he had suddenly changed his mind about the train to Domodossola. It wasn't a specially good explanation. It was true, in a sense, that he had been brought to a sudden standstill by a voice. But the voice was neither that of a mystic warning him to go

64

back nor of a guardian angel seeking to change the course of his destiny. He hadn't on the whole been very explicit about it, but it was the best he could do. The voice was really the voice of Miss Beaumont – not so much her speaking voice, in reality, as the voice communicating itself to him through the cool calm blue eyes – suddenly binding him in a compelling, instantaneous attraction.

When he reached the hotel he saw with considerable pleasure that Miss Beaumont was sitting on the terrace with the Bompiani children. The girl, who had been drinking coffee, looked splendidly fair, cool and bored as she stared at the lake below. The two little girls, who had been drinking orange juice, now greeted him with lips stained with bright yellow moustaches, shouting:

'Tricks! Tricks! Tricks! *Prego, prego!* Tricks!'

'Good afternoon.' He smiled with charm and friendliness at Miss Beaumont, who herself stared in answer. 'May I sit down?'

'Tricks! Tricks!'

'I suppose you wonder why I'm back. Absolutely impossible to resist the lake in this weather, that's all – I just couldn't resist it.' Miss Beaumont neither smiled nor made a comment. 'Don't you think it's beautiful?'

'I like Garda better.'

He started to do his tricks. He was, he thought, rather good with the tricks. Children always liked them. He had first taken up tricks and conjuring generally as a boy, and by now he had forgotten the best of them. But at home he still had the first box he had bought with his pocket money, still neatly packed away in his bedroom, after forty years. Among the tricks was a very good one by which you turned water into wine. There was also another in which you invited several people to write whatever they liked on a paper, seal it in an envelope and hand it to you. Then, one by one, you held the envelopes up to the light, concentrated for a few moments and then, before opening the envelope, told the audience exactly what they had written. It was always a tremendous, baffling success but of course you needed a collaborator.

On the table were a few wrapped cubes of sugar left over from Miss Beaumont's coffee. He palmed them, made a few mysterious dabs at the air and then produced them from the ears of the Bompiani little girls.

Shrieking with laughter, they broke into brief wild English:

'More! Again! More, more!'

'Ah! and now where? Now?'

Opening his hands, he revealed them both quite empty.

'Gone, you see, gone. Gone! – where?'

Baffled, as they always were, the little Bompiani children searched his inner sleeves. Deftly, in triumph, he produced the sugar from the side of Miss Beaumont's hair.

It was clear, in a moment, that Miss Beaumont did not think the trick either very successful or very amusing, but the little Bompiani angels danced with delight, half-hysterically.

'Freda! Freda! Freda!' they said.

'Ah! yes, that time it was Freda,' he said. 'Sugar in Freda's hair. But not now – not this time. This time in – !'

'Rosali! Rosali!'

To shrieking laughter he opened his hands and again they were empty.

'I'm afraid I've done this trick so many times it's getting stale,' he said.

'Yes,' Miss Beaumont said. 'I suppose it must be.'

'I'll have to think up new ones. I know several. It just needs thinking.'

'Yes.'

'Do you play tennis?' he suddenly said.

'Occasionally.'

'Oh! really! oh! fine. They have very good courts at the Splendide that you can hire. I wonder – '

'I haven't a racket.'

'I always bring two,' the major said. 'It would be awfully nice if you'd care to – perhaps tomorrow?'

'Tomorrow we go to Orta.'

'Well, there's plenty of time. How long are you here?'

She shrugged her shoulders.

'Three weeks. A month. I wouldn't know.'

'Then there's bags of time,' the major said. 'By the way the swimming is pretty good in the lake. The water's still warm. Do you –'

'Tricks! Tricks!' the children shrieked. 'Tricks!'

The insistent voices pierced the afternoon air wildly, maddening as discharging pop-guns.

'Tricks! Sugar in Freda's hair! Tricks!'

'Oh! my God, these kids,' the girl said. 'Three weeks of this will drive me batty.'

'Let's have a drink this evening somewhere,' the major said. 'We could nip down into the town –'

Before Miss Beaumont could answer, and as if by a process of telepathy, Miss Bentley appeared at the door of the hotel, calling the major by name, waving a handful of letters.

'Anything to post, Major Wilshaw?'

'No, I don't think so. Many thanks.'

'I'm walking to the town before dinner – I just wondered – nothing you want?'

He called no, nothing, thanking her all the same, and Miss Bentley called back:

'Are the children restless? Would they care to come?'

'May they really?' Miss Beaumont said. 'Isn't it an awful trouble?'

'Absolutely not.'

Miss Bentley, calling the little angels, held out both hands. Major Wilshaw called back something about his tricks being exhausted and how he would have to think up new ones and then remembered something else and said:

'Oh! there is just one thing you could do for me, Miss

Bentley. That's if it's no trouble. If you haven't too much to do yourself – '

'I'm picking up a couple of dresses, that's all,' Miss Bentley said. 'I must have something new if I'm to stay here another month.'

'Excuse me a moment,' the major said to Miss Beaumont. 'Don't run away.'

Walking across to Miss Bentley he stopped half-way, took from his pocket a fountain pen and notebook and wrote something down, afterwards tearing out the page.

'Just a telegram if you wouldn't mind. I think it'll be five hundred lire. Something like that – '

'Oh! not to worry now,' Miss Bentley said. 'I'll tell you at dinner – '

'Awfully kind of you, Miss Bentley. More than kind.'

'Not a bit,' she said. 'Come along, angels. No, no, no! Take care! Don't run into the road!'

Back at the table, sitting facing Miss Beaumont, looking into the cool prepossessing eyes, wonderfully blue and bored, the major felt run through him the first of a series of exciting, scurrying emotions and tried suddenly to disguise them by an appearance of casualness:

'She's an awfully decent old stick, really. Terribly kind. Quite witty too. Sits hours staring at the lake, dreaming. Quite happy, I suppose, wondering what she might have had – '

'And what might she have had?'

The major, unable to put into words what Miss Bentley might have had, suddenly felt obliged to change the subject and looked up at the hills.

'You can walk quite a way through the vineyards,' he said. 'There's an old back road goes up behind the hotel and you come out above the terraces. It's a magnificent view. Would you care to walk up?'

'Oh! it's awfully hot – '

'Still two hours before dinner,' the major said. 'There's

a little *trattoria* up the top where we could get a glass of wine.'

'I don't like wine,' the girl said. 'By golly, the time drags here. I thought it was later.'

By the time the major and Miss Beaumont had reached the upper terraces of vines, from which the view over the descending trellises of misty olive fruit was, as the major had said, so magnificent, Miss Bentley had reached the post office down in the town.

There, for the first time, she looked at the major's telegram.

'Please post soonest box conjuring tricks bottom left hand corner wardrobe dressing-room,' it read, 'regards Wilshaw.'

As the days went past Miss Bentley continued to sit on the terrace, watching the sky, the mountains, the lake and the steamers crossing the lake; watching too the oleanders still opening fresh sprays of white, pink, vermilion and yellow flower.

After a week or so the gathering of grapes began on the terraces above the hotel and all day she could hear the voices of workers calling, chattering and laughing across the vineyards. In mornings of exquisite light she watched the mountains emerge from shrouds of mist, mostly a pure ochreous bloom, occasionally pale rose and more rarely still a tender egg-shell green below which the distant houses looked more than ever like squat white candles gently melting; sometimes making in the mellow air the only visible division between land and water, just as the thin snow caps made the only perceptible division between land and sky.

She also watched Major Wilshaw. For the first few mornings he appeared on the terrace with his customary fresh briskness, immaculate. She saw him look with eagerness from table to table, searching for Miss Beaumont, who was never there. At the fourth morning he inquired for her.

'Miss Beaumont not down?'

'She never eats breakfast.'

'No?' He appeared startled, even shocked. 'Not eat breakfast? How –'

'She told me so.'

After that Major Wilshaw did not appear for breakfast either.

He would appear instead about eleven o'clock, carrying a towel, ready for his swim.

'Miss Beaumont not about?'

'Haven't seen her.'

'She was coming for a swim at eleven o'clock.' He glanced hurriedly at his watch, fretting. 'It's a quarter past already.'

'She hates getting up,' Miss Bentley said. 'There are people who do, you know.'

The major fretted until a quarter to twelve and then said:

'Damn. I hate missing my swim. I hate swimming by myself too.'

Miss Bentley did not answer but found herself looking obliquely, instead, at the small fresh pink ears. This glance seemed to startle the major into new thoughts and he said:

'I suppose you wouldn't care to come? No, I don't suppose –'

She smiled in her quizzical, rather ironic way.

'Are you asking me?'

'Oh yes – I'm sorry, Miss Bentley. Of course I am, of course.'

'Thank you. If you'll wait for me I'll get my costume.'

Ten minutes later they were walking down the steps of the terrace when Miss Beaumont appeared at the foot of them.

'Where on earth have you been?'

'Waiting,' the major said. 'Here on the terrace. Waiting. Have you only just – ?'

'I was here all the time,' Miss Beaumont said. She spoke frigidly. 'In the garden. In the garden was where you said.'

Humbled and confused, the major made groping attempts at apology, almost stuttering. Miss Beaumont, cooler than ever, more aloof and more distant, gazed into air. Miss Bentley said nothing but:

'Well, if we're going, shall we go?'

The figure of Miss Beaumont was virginal, slender and wiry, with small, sharp, up-pointed breasts. As she walked she held her shoulders well back, self-consciously, swinging her hands elaborately. The major, as the three of them walked down the hillside towards the lake, seemed stunned and mesmerized by this, keeping his eyes fixed on her in a stupor of admiration, not once glancing at Miss Bentley.

In the hot brilliant noon unexpected numbers of people were swimming in the lake or lying on concrete, below lines of bathing huts, sunning themselves.

As he saw them the major hurried forward, murmuring something about grabbing a cubicle before it was too late, and then came back, three or four minutes later, dismayed.

'Rather as I suspected,' he said. 'Only two huts left. Do you mind? – you will have to share I'm afraid. I'm awfully sorry –'

'Oh! that's all right,' Miss Beaumont said and stared away, glassily.

Only five minutes later the major saw a white-costumed Miss Bentley emerge first from the cubicle, smiling strangely. Sitting on warm concrete, he was dangling his legs above the lake and turned in time to see the smile break into open laughter.

'What are you laughing at?'

'Oh, nothing.'

'It seems to tickle you tremendously all the same.'

Once again Miss Bentley's strange smile broke into open laughter.

'Not going to share the joke?'

'Oh, it was nothing,' Miss Bentley said. 'It was just that I don't think Miss Beaumont liked sharing the cubicle, that's all. She's rather shy.'

Before the major could make up his mind what to say about

this Miss Bentley was lying full length on the concrete. With sensations of surprise and disbelief he found himself staring at her figure, relaxed and brown in its white two-piece suit in the sun. It was a remarkably taut, clean, smooth figure for a woman to whom, as he thought, he could give a few years. The legs were firm, hairless and shapely. The flesh on the rather long sloping shoulders was wonderfully clean and golden and the bust held itself upright, like that of a girl, self-supported.

Miss Bentley, who had closed her eyes for a moment or two against the brilliance of the sun, now opened them suddenly and found the major staring at her body. With warm, unsurprised, unequivocal eyes she looked straight back at him and said:

'By the way, I meant to have asked you. Have your tricks come?'

'No. I can't understand it. It's been nearly two weeks now. It's rather tiresome. The children keep pestering and I promise them every day.'

'Could they be held by the Customs?'

'Good gracious.' The thought had on Major Wilshaw the effect of revelation. 'I never thought of that.'

'I think you'll probably find that that's what's happened,' Miss Bentley said.

He was about to say something about what a genius she had for putting her finger on the solution to a problem when he turned and saw that Miss Beaumont had left the cubicle and was walking across to where he and Miss Bentley sat by the lakeside.

Seeing her, he was unaccountably depressed by an effect of flatness about the dark red costume. The legs were extraordinarily thin, like a boy's, and too hollow at the thighs. He experienced the impression that Miss Beaumont, who looked so arrestingly pretty in cool silk frocks, now looked meagre, a mere slice of a girl, skimpy. He was so uneasy that he could not think what had happened to her.

He stood up. At the same moment Miss Bentley stood up too, erect and full, her brown hair remarkably thick and bright against the golden sloping shoulders. Miss Beaumont was tying a red bathing hat on her head and this, as it enclosed her hair, made her look more than ever like a boy. Immature and white, her shoulders were awkwardly twisted, showing salt-cellars.

'Ah! there you are at last,' the major said. 'Ready?'

'There's no great hurry, is there?' she said.

With studied rapture Miss Bentley turned and stared into the tranquil heart of the lake, disturbed here and there only by the faintest silver ruffles, little islands of coat-of-mail that drifted, sparkled, took to air and floated away.

'Heavens, this lake looks as deep as the end of time this morning,' she said. 'Don't you think so? I've noticed it before on these, hot, still days.'

She turned to Miss Beaumont, whose toe-nails were painted red, giving her a still more unreal, doll-like appearance.

'I'll give you one guess how deep it is,' Miss Bentley said.

Miss Beaumont too gazed at the lake, silent, evidently not wanting to guess at its depth and giving once more, as a consequence, an impression of compressed virginal aloofness.

'Fourteen hundred feet they tell me,' Miss Bentley said.

A moment later she dived. As she did so Major Wilshaw realized that he had never seen her swim before. He had no idea whether she swam well or badly.

A second later he realized that she had totally disappeared. The great depth of the lake had swallowed her. In a stupefying moment of astonishment, followed by shock, he was pained by an unpleasant sensation. He was unaware of giving a gasp of alarm or of walking several paces towards the edge of the water and, at last, of letting out a half-choked breath, part in relief, part in sheer admiration, as Miss Bentley surfaced thirty yards away, turned belly-wise like a clean white fish and floated in the sun.

As his alarm drained away he turned to see Miss Beaumont sitting down.

'What was all the fuss about?'

'Fuss? Oh, nothing. I just wondered when – Aren't you coming in?'

'Not yet,' the girl said. 'I'm rather chilly. I'll lie in the sun.'

He turned from the flat figure to face a sun that, even at the angle of October, sliced at his eyes with clear hot brightness. A moment later he dived and swam slowly and unhurriedly out to where Miss Bentley floated, face upwards, perfectly still.

To his fresh surprise she again had on her face the strange smile that had mystified him a few minutes before.

'No idea you swam so well.'

She did not answer. Instead, for the second or third time, the smile broke into actual laughter.

'Oh! look, aren't you going to share this joke with me?'

'Some jokes make you laugh more when you don't share them,' Miss Bentley said. 'They sort of evaporate when you start telling.'

'I've got an idea it's about me,' he said.

'Oh! good lord no.'

'About Miss Beaumont then?'

Again she did not answer and he knew now that the joke, whatever it was, was about Miss Beaumont.

He paddled water. Small brilliant pearls of water lay in the hollow above Miss Bentley's breasts. She kept her hands flicking, fin-like, at full length and the smile on her face did not fade.

'Might just as well tell me.'

'I don't think it would be fair on Miss Beaumont.'

It suddenly amused her to tease the major and with lazy strokes she started swimming on her back, towards a diving raft that lay fifteen yards away. He followed at a slow crawl, keeping some distance behind.

74

On the raft two muscular, good-looking Italians, about twenty or so, sleek, with black hair, walnut bodies and brief blue swimming trunks, watched her come in, heave herself to the raft and sit dripping in the sun. She lifted herself aboard the raft in one easy swinging movement and the Italians smiled across at each other as the major followed, heaving himself up with difficulty, in several puffing movements, his own weight too much for him, so that in the end Miss Bentley stretched out and gave him a hand.

'Funny how I've never seen you down at the Lido before.' the major said. 'How did you get so brown?'

'You always come in the mornings,' Miss Bentley said. 'I always come in the afternoons, when you're napping. I have lunch earlier than you.'

She turned and lay on her back, wet hair spread outwards, and the two Italians stared at her full, prostrate body as it glittered in the sun.

The major lay down too and after five minutes or so turned his head, saw that her eyes were closed and said:

'Going to swim any more?'

'I think so, yes. And you?'

'I don't think so. I think I'll lie in the sun.'

A moment or two later she dived, came up only a few yards away and started to swim with an easy crawl along the path of the sun. Almost immediately she had dived the taller, older of the two young Italians dived too and swam with long strokes after her.

Miss Bentley, turning some moments later to float on her back, found him smiling brilliantly alongside her.

'Hullo.'

'Hullo,' she said.

'Hot today.' His smile was very white. A crucifix glittered gold on the wet black hairs of his chest. 'Are you thirsty?'

'Not very. Why?'

'I thought if you thirsty you have drink with me?'

Miss Bentley smiled, lapping water with outstretched fingers.

'That sounds nice. Did the other one dare you?'

'Did what? *Prego?*'

'Oh! it doesn't matter. Where do you drink anyway?'

He pointed shorewards with a very brown, very well-manicured hand.

'At the little caffè at the end of the Lido. Just there. You take coffee, vermouth, what you like. Oh! him?' he said, pointing back to the raft. 'He's my brother.'

Miss Bentley, not answering at once, turned to see where the major was. She discovered him to be sitting upright on the raft, watching her. The sight of him sitting there gave her so much satisfaction that she smiled again and then turned, still smiling, to the Italian boy.

'I don't think my friend would like it.'

'No? You have to ask him?'

'No, but –'

She gave him the kind of glance that Major Wilshaw often found quizzical, sometimes ironical, but not really coquettish, and the boy seemed to find it so attractive that he swam closer.

'Then will you come?'

'I don't think so. I think my friend would be very jealous. I think he wouldn't like it.'

'Jealous?' the boy said. 'It's very good to be jealous. That's good.'

She felt his hand brush itself quickly across her back.

'He's watching. Another thing – You're much too close to me.'

'Of course,' he said. 'If I didn't want to be close to you I would be sitting on the raft. Like your friend.'

Slowly and boldly his eyes travelled the full length, from hair to toes, of her floating body.

'Will you come now?' he said. 'They have very good *orvieto* at the caffè. After the swim it very good –'

'Supposing I preferred coffee?'

'Very well, then. Good. Coffee! –'

He smiled handsomely, brilliantly again, with vanity, pleased with himself. 'I suppose he does it every day,' she told herself and smiled too.

As they swam shorewards together he kept very close to her and once or twice he touched her arm, but she did not protest or move away. Nor did she once look back to where a stunned Major Wilshaw, squatting on the raft with his arms huddled across his knees, was staring at her across the tranquil surface of the lake, solemnly, with disbelieving eyes.

It was after five o'clock when she was sitting on the patio, drinking tea with slices of lemon in it, and Major Wilshaw appeared. It was the first time she had seen him since midday and now he was carrying a parcel in his hands.

'You were quite right about the tricks,' he said. 'There was a mess-up about a customs form. Cost me another five hundred lire but anyway I've got them now.'

'The children will be thrilled.'

The major continued to stand by her table, a little coolly, as if purposely intending not to sit down.

'Won't you have some tea?' Miss Bentley said. 'We could easily ask for another cup.'

'I had a cup in the town.'

He shifted uneasily from one foot to another, at the same time changing the parcel from hand to hand.

'You disappeared rather quickly all of a sudden this morning,' he said.

'Oh! did I?'

'I thought it was rather swift.'

She played with a slice of lemon in her cup, submerging it and poking at it thoughtfully with a spoon.

'I didn't want to play gooseberry,' she said, 'that's all.'

'I don't know about gooseberry.'

She did not answer; she drank tea instead and the major went on:

'After all, the three of us went down together and I naturally thought – You didn't come back to lunch, either, did you?'

'No,' she said. 'I had lunch at the caffè.'

'Oh?' he said. 'With the two Italian boys?'

'With one of them.'

She looked up as she said this and she thought the face of the major flushed.

'He's rather nice,' she said. 'And I think rather well off too. His father makes motor tyres.'

The major, lifting his head suddenly, made a quick short noise of expiration, somewhere between a snort and a sigh.

'What was all that in aid of?' Miss Bentley said.

'Nothing. Only I didn't think you were a pick-up.'

'Of course it was a pick-up.' She said this with deliberate emphasis and it amused her to see his face as she teased him.

'Well!' he said. 'Well!'

'What's wrong with a pick-up?' she said. 'After all, thousands of women all over the world are simply longing for a pick-up. It's all they dream about. Every night. Every day.'

'Yes, but really I must say it's rather surprising in *you*, isn't it?' the major said. 'And with – with this boy.'

'Why with me? And why not with a boy? After all,' she said, 'you have your Miss Beaumont.'

'That's rather different.'

'Is it?' she said. 'I don't see how. Miss Beaumont and the Italian boy are about the same age as each other. So are you and I.'

'Yes, but I mean. With an older woman and a young –'

He broke off suddenly, unable to complete the sentence in which he was clearly going to say that he thought that when women of her age chose to consort with young men of twenty it was something rather cheap, unladylike and distasteful. After this he stood stiffly, almost to attention, with an air of offence, not speaking.

'I'm sorry if I made you angry.'

'Oh! you didn't make me angry.' She looked up to see a flush of anger on his face and felt extraordinarily pleased that it was there. 'Not a bit.'

Pleasantly, coolly and without haste, aware of the major's discomfort, she poured herself another cup of tea, put sugar and lemon into it and stirred it delicately with her spoon.

'What about the tricks?' she said. 'Will you do them to-night?'

'That's really what I wanted to see you about,' the major said. He relaxed a little. He even allowed himself the beginnings of a short stiff smile. 'You see it's slightly awkward – '

'In what way?'

'Well, in at least one of the tricks, probably two, I need a collaborator and I rather thought – '

'Wouldn't Miss Beaumont do?'

'Oh! no, no, no, no. I don't think so. You see – '

'When is all this going to be?' Miss Bentley said and again she turned on him her slightly quizzical, slightly ironical smile. 'This trickery and collaboration?'

'I thought if we rehearsed a bit we could do it by tomorrow night.'

She drank the remainder of her tea. And then, wiping her lips and the tips of her fingers with a paper serviette, which she afterwards crumpled up in her hands, she came to a sudden decision which astounded herself.

'I'm afraid I can't tomorrow,' she said. 'I'm driving into Pallanza to have dinner with this young man.'

She looked up suddenly to see the effect of her words on the major and found his face unexpectedly blank and the colour of greyish cardboard.

'I see,' he said and then turned suddenly and walked away across the terrace and into the hotel, leaving her staring at the lake, across the pink-blue surface of which a steamer was cutting, like a white knife, a path against the sun.

Suddenly, as he disappeared, she was aware of feeling uneasy, no longer so confident in herself. The tea and the lemon abruptly started to repeat themselves and she knew that if she were not very careful they would bring on an uncomfortable attack of heartburn.

The following evening, shortly before seven o'clock, she started to walk into the town. As she went down the steps of the hotel Major Wilshaw appeared suddenly from the garden, almost as if he had been waiting in hiding, hoping to catch her.

'I thought you were driving to Pallanza.'

'So I am. But something happened to the boy's car and he said would I walk to meet him.'

The major stood awkwardly, first on one foot, then the other. She thought he combined an appearance of great smartness with considerable uneasiness as he fingered the lapel of his suit of navy blue mohair. A little cream handkerchief showed triangular-wise from the breast pocket. He fingered that too and said:

'Actually Miss Beaumont and I are dining out too. It's nice to have a change sometimes.'

'Oh! Where?'

'At the Splendide. We can dance there.'

She moved to go away.

'Oh! about the tricks,' he said.

'Yes?'

'I've got it all fixed for tomorrow. I want to do it properly. Signora Fascioli says I can use the writing-room. Of course I shall invite her.'

'Naturally.'

He suddenly made such a mess of fingering the handkerchief that he pulled it out in entirety, together with a small silver pencil, which fell on the steps.

'That wasn't very clever,' he said, without laughing. 'I'll have to do better than that.'

She began to feel highly uneasy herself as he stooped to pick up the pencil.

'Well, I'll have to fly now,' she said. 'I'll be late otherwise.'

Fumbling hopelessly with pencil and handkerchief he said:

'What I wanted to say was would you? – you know, just help a bit? – tomorrow?'

'If you think I'd be any good.'

'Of course, of course. Thank you. Well, I mustn't keep you –'

She hurried away, not looking back. She kept up a quick pace for a hundred yards or so and then fell into a slow, dawdling walk. Across the lake, where the sun had already set, an orange-green glow, touched with purple, lay softly on the more distant water. The mountains above it were also purple, except at the tips. There they were pink-amber in the afterglow, and along the shore and in the valleys the lights of towns were coming on.

In the town she bought an English newspaper. Then she went into a small side-street restaurant and ordered an omelette and made it last as long as she could. In the paper she read, as she sipped at a glass of *valpolicella*, that the weather in London was unusually cold for mid-October. Snow had already fallen in the Cairngorm mountains of Scotland. An actress she had once seen in a play had died from an overdose of sleeping tablets. Some shares she held in rubber had fallen six points or so.

After the omelette she ordered cheese and fruit. Then, because there were many grapes on the dish, both green and black ones, she made the cheese and fruit last almost twice as long as the omelette had done. By that time she had read most of the things in the paper.

Afterwards she ordered coffee and sat for some time trying

to work out how long it would take anyone to drive to Pallanza, have dinner at leisure and drive back again. She supposed that she ought to add to this another half an hour, or even more, for saying good-night to a young, handsome and easy-spoken Italian with plenty of energy, money and time to spare and she decided it would be at least eleven o'clock before she dare be seen walking up the steps of the hotel, where on hot nights guests often sat until midnight, talking.

By this time it was only nine o'clock and she ordered a brandy with fresh coffee and started to do the crossword in the newspaper. The words of the crossword did not come to her very easily. She found herself thinking of Major Wilshaw and Miss Beaumont and what dinner might be like at the Splendide and if the band was good for dancing. She smiled once into space as she remembered the incident in the bathing cubicle when she and Miss Beaumont were undressing together but the waiter misinterpreted the smile as a gesture that she wanted him and came over, bowing, and said:

'Yes, signora? Is something you wanted?'

'Just the bill,' she said and wondered miserably what had made her say so.

As she walked slowly back along the promenade by the lakeside the night was extraordinarily warm and still and she could sometimes catch the faint vanilla-like scent of oleanders blooming under the street-lights, about the path.

Then a hundred yards away from the entrance to the Splendide she saw the unmistakable figure of Major Wilshaw, with Miss Beaumont, leave the hotel, cross the street and come straight towards her.

In panic she turned completely round, walked back several yards and hid behind a clump of oleanders, from which she pretended to be gazing, with her face in her hands, at the lights of Pallanza, several miles away. As the major and Miss Beaumont passed her she heard the major say, without drawing any answer from Miss Beaumont:

'I should like to have had little invitation cards printed. Fun for the children, I thought. But then of course, there isn't time and I'll have to write them.'

As they passed out of hearing Miss Bentley suddenly hated herself for the stupid evening she had spent and then hated Miss Beaumont even more for not responding with a single word to the major's charming thought.

The major walked on with Miss Beaumont until they came to a caffè where, between small candle-lit tables, a two-piece orchestra consisting of piano and piano accordion were playing. Dinner at the Splendide had been taken in a large, echoing, chandeliered room in which the seven waiters had outnumbered the guests by two and there had been, because of the lateness of the season, no dancing.

One of the things the major had discovered he disliked most in life was dancing on a floor, between very small tables, measuring perhaps six feet by four, and he began to think with envy of Miss Bentley, dining quietly at Pallanza, perhaps under one of those charming arbours of vines so common to Italy, or under a canopy of trained chestnut branches.

'Oh! this is fun,' Miss Beaumont said. 'I feel like sticking a candle in your hair.'

'Oh, please don't.'

'Oh, come on,' she said. 'Take your back hair down. Have fun. Somebody told me this is the place where they dance on the tables.'

The two-piece band poured music down his throat from a distance of two yards like a blast from a furnace door. The hard thin body of Miss Beaumont flung him from side to side. Her breasts pressed against him with the hardness of two shapely little Easter eggs and now and then she chanted into his ear, in an abrasive voice, the brittle, chirpy words of songs she knew.

'And relax, relax,' she said. 'Let your feet go. Your bones are set. Let your feet go.'

Some time later they were served with a luke-warm soup

that looked like porridge and that the major discovered, with violent distaste, was made entirely of garlic, finely shredded. With difficulty and wretchedness he ate several spoonfuls, washing it down with sharp red wine, and wondered miserably how long his breath would smell.

'Glorious fun,' Miss Beaumont said. 'Come on, you old candlestick, dance with me.'

Later, towards eleven o'clock, a young Italian girl danced on a table, to be joined presently by one of the waiters. Miss Beaumont climbed on a table and started dancing too, kicking her thin legs, shouting to the major to join her. The table was not large enough for two and he succeeded in getting up on another, but some moments later the table suddenly collapsed and the major fell heavily, bruising his shin against a chair. When he tried to dance again the garlic, quarrelling already with the wine, started repeating violently, making him belch, and he felt strong waves of hot nausea begin to rise.

When Miss Beaumont came down from the table and danced with him on the floor again she said:

'What on earth are you hobbling for?'

'I barked my shin. It's rather painful.'

'Oh! rub it with brandy!' she said. 'You won't die.'

After that they drank more red wine, followed by a sweet liqueur tasting strangely of perfumed oranges. It too quarrelled with the garlic and soon a painful area of burning, deep and formidable, settled about the major's chest.

As he drove Miss Beaumont home in a taxi, soon after one o'clock, he could not decide if she were tipsy, happy or merely excited, but suddenly he decided to interpret her mood as one in which, at all costs, she longed for him to kiss her.

To his surprise, as his hands touched her body, she pushed him away.

'If you're going to kiss me, kiss me,' she said. 'Don't creep all over me.'

84

The major, who had no intention of creeping all over her and who also flattered himself that he was capable of reasonable behaviour, did not know what to say. The attempt to kiss her, when he made it at last, was not successful, partly because, perhaps for the twentieth or thirtieth time, the garlic again began to rise.

Up in his room the major discovered, after an hour, that he could not sleep at all. The garlic, the sharp red wine, the strange orange liqueur and a repetitive taste of a portion of scampi he had eaten at dinner quarrelled with continual violence just above his heart.

He got up at last, switched on the light and unpacked the box of tricks that had given him so much pleasure as a boy. He decided to put in some practice on the tricks but after some moments he discovered that he had, over the years, forgotten most of them, particularly the one where he needed the collaboration of Miss Bentley.

Depressed and worn out, he went to the window and stared at the diminishing number of lights on the shores of the lake below. As he stood there a car drew up outside, its door banged, and he looked down to see a woman alighting.

Though the woman was in fact Signora Fascioli coming home late from visiting her eldest sister in Arona he was sure, in the darkness, that it was Miss Bentley, at last returning from Pallanza.

The thought depressed him more than ever. He experienced a pitiful moment of jealousy and then decided he hated himself as much as Miss Bentley. The garlic began to rise again and he drank several glasses of water, together with three aspirins, before going back to bed, to lie there miserably wondering how many coffee beans he would have to chew in the morning before he was again a civilized, presentable man.

The following evening, after dinner, the major put on his little performance of tricks in the writing room. He had gone to the trouble of writing out little cards of invitation, which the Bompiani children clutched with delight and on which he described himself as *Major Paulo: the Magic Wanderer*. He had remembered in time that he had called himself *the Magic Wanderer* as a boy. It was still rather good, he thought. The *Major Paulo* was an afterthought and because of it Miss Bentley grasped, for the first time, that his name was Paul.

The Bompiani family, with Miss Bentley, Miss Beaumont, Signora Fascioli, Maria, Enrico and the two cooks sat in rows of chairs. The major had the tricks set out on a table covered with a red cloth he had borrowed from Signora Fascioli. He had rehearsed the tricks very hard during the late morning and afternoon and he had let Miss Bentley into the necessary secrets of collaboration. She seemed in some way subdued, her enthusiasm restricted, he thought, but he hoped things would go very well all the same.

When he appeared, bowed and took up his magic wand the Bompiani family led the applause and the children stood up, clapping and dancing.

'Thank you, thank you,' he said. 'Thank you. Now, ladies and gentlemen, *signori e signore*, if you will let me have your kind attention, a few examples of the magic art –'

Miss Beaumont stared with stony eyes. Miss Bentley felt unaccountably nervous, still despising herself. The Bompiani children shrieked far too much, she thought, and the whisperings of Maria and one of the cooks, in local Italian, got on her nerves.

The major first did a trick where he turned water into wine. That always went well. He was pleased that there were many 'Bravos!' mostly led by Signor Bompiani and taken up by the two little angels in a chanting chorus. After this he did a trick in which he made a fool's cap of thick white paper, poured a glass of milk into it and then abruptly screwed up the empty fool's cap and threw it away. That went very well too and again there was much applause, many 'Bravos!' and much admiring laughter. Before, during and after each trick he waved his magic wand.

After several other tricks, including one in which he cut a thick silk rope in half and joined it together again, and then a piece of baffling illusion with a black box, the time came for him to collaborate with Miss Bentley.

'For this trick I also need the collaboration of the audience,' he said, 'Signor Bompiani – perhaps you would be good enough to translate please?'

Signor Bompiani, who had a melodious, easy voice, translated at some length, so that by the time he had finished Miss Bentley felt more unsure of herself than ever. She found herself wanting the trick to succeed even more than the major did and she began to be afraid that the two cooks, who looked dopey as they listened, did not understand.

'It is all very simple,' the major said. 'You will each write whatever you like on a piece of paper, put the paper into an envelope and then seal it down. Please remember what you have written, because I shall then take each envelope *and*, *without opening it*, tell you what it is.'

'We write in Italian or English?' Signora Fascioli said.

'Whichever you like,' the major said. 'But in Italian only the simple words!'

Miss Beaumont, who looked more distant than ever, was seen to dash off a single word. Signor Bompiani wrote three pieces, one each for the little angels. The cooks and Enrico sucked their pencils. Someone was heard distinctively to say *O! Sole Mio* and behind Miss Bentley there were sudden reproving cat-like hissings.

The major collected the envelopes. As he collected them he chattered a good deal, in traditional conjuring fashion, distracting attention and at the same time creating an air of expectancy.

'Now!' he said. 'I am ready to read your minds. Envelope Number One!'

He stared with intensity, for twenty seconds or so, at the first

87

envelope, holding it up to the light of the central chandelier.

'I think,' he said at last, 'yes, I think I penetrate the veil of the first mind. I think I know what words this envelope contains. Yes!' He spoke slowly, passing his hands in mystical, groping fashion in front of his eyes. 'I think – yes, I am sure.' With drama, flourishing the envelope, he proclaimed: 'I think the words this envelope contains are "The spring in the mountains".' He paused. 'Did anyone write that?'

The major had arranged with Miss Bentley that at this point there should be a dramatic pause: almost as if the trick, in its first moment, had failed. Miss Bentley, as she heard her own words read out, felt her throat become harsh and dry. She was unable to frame her words. She felt as if years went by before she was able to say, quietly:

'Yes. I wrote *the spring in the mountains*.'

The major made a gesture of modest triumph. There was again much applause. 'Bravo! Bravo!' everyone said and Signor Bompiani exclaimed in round, melodious English: 'Jolly good, major. Jolly good.'

While this was going on the major swiftly tore open the envelope, memorized its contents and picked up the next one. Holding it up to the light he suddenly said:

'Ah! I know what you are saying. You are saying that when I hold the envelope up to the light the envelope becomes transparent. That is not so. Signor Bompiani – would you oblige? Take the envelope please and hold it up to the light. Is the envelope transparent or not?'

Signor Bompiani took the envelope and held it up to the light.

'Thick as London fog,' he said. 'Can't see a blooming thing.'

'Thank you, sir,' the major said. There was some laughter. One of the cooks giggled. The two Bompiani angels started giggling too. 'Yes, this one I think is easy. Did someone write *God Save the Queen*?'

'Guilty,' Signor Bompiani said. 'I wrote it for this one,' and picked up the younger of the two children and put her on his knee.

'Bravo!' everyone said, with applause. 'Bravo!'

The trick, Miss Bentley thought, was going quite well after all. The worst, she felt, was over. She sucked her lips in relief, feeling saliva flow warmly down to her throat, melting the dry harshness there. She had now no more to do except listen and during the next few moments she heard Signora Fascioli confess to have written, in English, *There'll always be an England*, and Signor Bompiani, also in English, to *A nice cup of tea*. It was Enrico who had written *O Sole Mio* after all.

Suddenly it seemed to Miss Bentley that the major grew uneasy. After Enrico's *O Sole Mio* he seemed all at once to lose buoyancy. She thought he looked irritated, flushed and a little under pressure.

'This envelope contains only a single word,' he said in a slow voice, at last. '*Candlestick*. Did someone write that? *Candlestick?*'

'I did,' Miss Beaumont said.

'Thank you,' the major said. His voice carried a thin, restrained note of sarcasm. 'Thank you.'

From that moment the trick began to go wrong. Miss Bentley sat watching the major's small pink ears flush to a dark, bruised red. After the neat envelope he paused, looked very confused, said something about 'it's very hard to concentrate on this one. I have to confess this one is very difficult', and then looked into the audience and said:

'Was there someone who didn't write *anything*?'

No one answered.

'Signor Bompiani.'

Signor Bompiani translated. One of the cooks raised her hand and said something. The Italians laughed and Signor Bompiani translated what the cook had said.

'She wrote nothing, she says. She says she hadn't time to think. She requires a lot of time for thinking.'

The major made a regretful gesture of resignation and said the spell was broken. The children, who had not understood the trick in the first place, looked more than ever mystified, and the major consoled them into fresh delight and giggling by producing round, bright pink sweets from their hair.

'Shame!' Signor Bompiani said. 'Won't you go on? It was marvellous.'

'It is too difficult now,' the major said. 'The spell is broken.'

'Still, it was marvellous,' Signor Bompiani said. Starting to applaud, he looked for approval towards his wife, who smiled also. 'Marvellous!' she said with her handsome, fat, velvety lips and applauded too.

'I can't think how you do it, Major,' Signor Bompiani said and then everyone said 'Marvellous!' or 'Bravo!' and clapped their hands.

Only Miss Beaumont, Miss Bentley noticed, did not clap her hands. Instead she took out her lipstick and touched up her lips and while the major did a final trick of pulling unending streams of coloured paper from his mouth, Miss Bentley, watching her, wondered what *Candlestick* meant and why it had offended the major into sarcasm. She supposed Miss Beaumont in turn wondered what *The spring in the mountains* meant and she hardly knew herself what had made her choose the words. They had come to her suddenly, in a moment of mysterious enlightenment, in the odd way that things sometimes do, without thought or premeditation.

She discovered suddenly that she had been lost in a little daydream in which her eyes had been fixed once again on Major Wilshaw's ears. Hastily she re-focused her eyes to find that Signor Bompiani was making a little speech, partly of thanks and partly, as it turned out, of invitation.

'On behalf of you all I thank the major most profoundly for a wonderful treat – is that the word? – treat? Yes? A great treat, Major, thank you.' The audience, led by Signor Bompiani, applauded once again. 'And now, something else. The Bompianis, I am sad to say, must go back to Milano the day after tomorrow.'

'Oh, no. No, no,' the major said. 'That's too bad.'

'Work. One must work,' Signor Bompiani said. 'Still, what about a picnic? A farewell, final picnic? Tomorrow?'

While Signor Bompiani was saying this Signora Fascioli slipped out of the room, beckoning Enrico, Maria and the two cooks to go with her.

'What do you say? Where shall we go? Where we went before? – to the place in the mountains?'

'Splendid,' the major said. 'Couldn't be better.'

'Good,' Signor Bompiani said. 'The only trouble is that we are one more this time. That makes it more difficult for the car.'

'It's easy to hire another car,' Miss Bentley said. 'The major and I would stand for that.'

Miss Beaumont suddenly spoke for only the second time.

'Or you could ask your Italian boy-friend along,' she said. 'That would even up the party. He has a car.'

Before Miss Bentley could recover from annoyance and astonishment Signor Bompiani was saying:

'Oh! Oh! Boy-friend? Miss Bentley? – an *Italian* boy-friend?'

'We simply had a swim together.'

'Oh?' Miss Beaumont said. 'I'm sorry. I thought it was lunch. And dinner too.'

Miss Bentley suddenly found herself in a hideous trap, not knowing what to answer. She was saved by Signor Bompiani, who laughed melodiously and said with generosity:

'Well, of course, invite him. The car would be most useful. It would be fun. What is his name? Perhaps we know him? Do you know his name?'

'I think his name is Balzari,' Miss Bentley said. 'His father manufactures motor-car tyres. But we –'

'Of course we know him! Very well. Of course. Balzari.

They have a villa here. Which boy is this? – the elder or the younger? There are two brothers.'

'I think his name is Vittorio –'

'Vittorio – the elder one. The other one is named Carlo, of course,' Signor Bompiani said. 'Nice boys. I shall telephone him myself.'

He began to take charge of the party, talking generously of drinks, occasionally saying 'Let's all have a nice cup of tea,' his favourite joke about the English, shepherding everyone forward to the patio, where little green and crimson lights were hung about the arbours of trellis work. Miss Bentley took the opportunity of hurrying ahead, murmuring about the need for her wrap and how she would get it from upstairs. The Bompiani angels clung to the major, one at each hand, with their mother just behind, leaving Signor Bompiani and Miss Beaumont to come from the writing-room last, together.

'Well, Freda, that was nice, eh?' He patted Miss Beaumont in a friendly way on the shoulder. 'Didn't you enjoy that? Didn't you think the trick with the envelopes was a good one? I can't think how the major does it at all.'

'I know how it's done,' Miss Beaumont said. 'It's as old as the hills.'

Upstairs, in her room, where the lights of the lake shining through the slats of the Venetian blinds made cage-like bars on the white ceiling, Miss Bentley sat looking at her quivering, foolish hands.

For the picnic lunch there were large piles of cold pork and salami, pink stacks of ham, two dishes of pâté, a whole *Bel Paese*, large nests of hard-boiled eggs, much bread and two baskets of fruit, mostly green and black grapes, with a few last blue figs and big butter-coloured pears. There were four flasks of Valpolicelli to drink, with white vermouth for those who preferred it, and mineral water for the angels. Miss Bentley and Signora Bompiani separated the slices of meat and laid them thickly on rounds of buttered bread. Miss Beaumont tied bibs on the children while Signor Bompiani and Vittorio, the Italian boy, who to Miss Bentley's relief had driven up with the major in his car, opened and poured out the wine. All across the mountains a still sharp light lay wonderfully distilled above the distances, with pure noon transparence, and the lake, more than ever like a pale blue glass lioness, was clearly visible below.

'Shall we drink to our meeting next summer?' Signor Bompiani said. Gaily he raised his glass to everybody; the wine glowed with a brilliant heart of fire in the sun. 'Let's drink to that, shall we?'

'Cheers,' the major said. '*Salut. Santé.* And everything else besides. To next year.'

Everyone drank wine as they sat about on short grass burned to bleached matting by the long summer. From somewhere higher up the slope, among the rocks, the sound of a spring breaking and beginning to run down the mountainside was the only sound in the fresh bright air except the sound of voices.

'Will you come back next year, Major?'

'My goodness I hope so.'

'And what about you, Miss Bentley?'

Miss Bentley, caught unawares by the question, did not know what to say.

'I may do,' she said. 'I shall see – '

'Or perhaps you prefer Pallanza?' Miss Beaumont said.

Looking up suddenly at this remark, Major Wilshaw saw on Miss Bentley's face something he had never seen there before. She had totally lost her look of assurance. Her expression was one of indecisive, rather helpless pain and suddenly it hurt him to see it there.

'Well, Pallanza is very nice,' Signor Bompiani said. 'But not so nice as this. What do you say, Vittorio? You like Pallanza?'

'No. Pallanza's noisy,' the boy said.

In panic Miss Bentley wondered how long the conversation

would go on but the major said quickly, changing the subject almost desperately, that he thought the nicest place he had seen in all Italy was a little town in one of the steep river valleys between Bolzano and Venice. Tobacco grew all along the sides of the valley and he thought it was very lovely there.

'Stupid of me, though,' he said. 'I can't even remember the name of it now.'

'Ah, Venice,' Signor Bompiani said. 'Venice.' He turned to the boy. 'Vittorio really comes from Venice, don't you?'

'My family has a house there.'

Part of a slice of ham hung down from the astonished lips of Miss Beaumont as she heard this. Her eyes fixed themselves on Vittorio Balzari with unbelief, fascination and with less coolness than she reserved for Miss Bentley and Major Wilshaw. Then she became aware of the pink trembling piece of ham dangling from her lips and pushed it hastily in and said:

'You have three houses? One in Milan, one in Venice, and one here?'

'Four, really,' he said. 'My mother has a flat in Rome too.'

Miss Beaumont swallowed her ham and tried to look as if, every day of her life, she heard of people who had houses in each of four illustrious and beautiful towns in Italy.

'How nice,' she said. 'Don't you find it hard to get servants for all these places?'

'No,' he said. 'In Italy we have plenty.'

'How many do you need for four houses?' Miss Beaumont said.

'I think we have twenty-seven – no, twenty-eight – waiters,' he said.

Everyone laughed at this, especially the three English, who were delighted at the misuse of the word waiters. Even Miss Bentley laughed. The major was quick to notice on her face a little break in the veil of pained, indecisive tension. He was glad he had been skilful in changing the subject of Pallanza.

Through the rest of the lunch he found himself looking more and more at her face, which from his lower position on the slope appeared to him framed completely against the sky, clear sharp blue above the mountains. And presently he found that he was looking at her, though he did not realize it at first, with tenderness. He felt he suddenly wanted to leave the pleasant arena of the laughing picnic and walk with Miss Bentley somewhere farther up the slopes, among the rocks, in complete solitude, where the spring rose.

Then he remembered the sentence she had written for the trick, *The spring in the mountains*, and he wondered what could have made her write the words. She had been very quiet, almost without a word, throughout the entire picnic. Now a puff of breeze had blown a few strands of her brown hair down across her forehead and eyes and in preoccupation she had not pushed it back again. He watched this brown curl of hair with new fascination and thought it gave her a certain lightness, a prettiness, he had never seen there before.

Then he was aware of Vittorio filling up his glass again and Signor Bompiani, who loved any excuse for drinking and even more for proposing a toast, raised his glass to everyone again and said:

'We have already drunk to next year. Now let's drink to this year. It's been wonderful.'

Everyone drank and agreed it had been wonderful.

'And to our English friends.'

'Thank you. And to our Italian friends.'

'Thank you, Major. Most kind.'

'And to the children. Our little angels,' the major said. 'If only we could all grow up so beautiful.'

Everyone laughed at the ambiguity of this remark, which Signor Bompiani translated for his wife, and Miss Beaumont said, 'Thank you,' with the faintest, most distant touch of sarcasm.

Then the two children suddenly raised their glasses of

mineral water and drank too, to the amusement of everybody, and there were fresh shrieks of laughter.

'Any more ham?' Signor Bompiani said. 'No more ham? No more salami? No more cheese? No, no, not for me.' He laughed loudly. 'If I eat more I must take too much shut-eye!'

As the major watched Miss Bentley quietly peeling a ripe fig and then sucking the light pink flesh from the broken purple balloon of skin he made up his mind that he would, somehow, get her to walk with him, after lunch, farther up the mountain-side. His only fear was that Vittorio would ask her first and again he felt a stab of jealousy about the boy and the journey to Pallanza, which had ended with the miserable fiasco of Miss Beaumont, the garlic and the incident of the candlestick, that blistering, sarcastic, crushing word.

Then he saw, after a time, that Signor Bompiani and his wife were already asleep among the rocks. The children were resting too, stretched out in the sun. Miss Bentley and Miss Beaumont were packing up the picnic things, disdaining help from men, though Vittorio was hovering near them: waiting, the major hoped, for Miss Beaumont to be free.

For five minutes he wandered away among the rocks, hoping that when he got back again Miss Bentley would be alone. When he did get back she was alone but, like the Bompianis, already lying down among the rocks, in the sun, with eyes closed.

He lay down too, the sun hot on his face, the air powdery dry with a smell of thin autumnal earth long burned by sum-mer. There was not a sound in the air except the sharp falling water of the spring rising invisibly, some distance up the gorge, from the rocks. Vittorio and Miss Beaumont had wandered away too and even the children did not stir.

He found he could not close his eyes at all. For a long time, lying face sideways, he watched Miss Bentley. The strand of hair had fallen down, for a second time, across her face. He wondered again what had happened at Pallanza to make her so unhappy and why she had written the words about the spring.

Suddenly she opened her eyes and lay there looking at him. He stared back at her without a flicker. Her eyes had no movement either. Her stare was profound, enraptured and mute and for a long time the two of them lay there in a trance, looking at each other, never moving, in air so quiet that the major could separate each sound of falling water from the other as clearly as notes on a flute.

It was a spell he never wanted to be broken but the children, leaping up suddenly, broke it with laughter. Hearing them, the Bompianis woke too and Signor Bompiani said:

'Well, did you sleep, Major? I dreamed I was the owner of a banana plantation on some island somewhere. How do you account for that? Too much salami and cheese I suppose.'

A few minutes later Vittorio and Miss Beaumont came back: Miss Beaumont, the major thought, looked thinly haughty; Vittorio rather baffled. Seeing them, Signor Bompiani said he was glad they were back. The air was far up and so late in the year got cold very quickly. For the children's sake they ought to go.

Two minutes later, although it was only three o'clock, the sun dipped behind a bastion of westerly mountainside, leaving a sheet of cold purple shadow through which the sound of spring water seemed suddenly to fall with iciness.

'Time for a nice cup of tea!' Signor Bompiani said: his favourite joke about England.

He led the way down the mountainside, carrying the younger child. The major carried the other angel and the rest followed, single file, with the picnic baskets.

At the foot of the path, just before they reached the cars, Signor Bompiani turned and called back:

'By the way, Major, when do you leave?'

'Not sure. I've stayed over three weeks longer than I meant already.'

Signor Bompiani turned again and called back.

'What about you, Miss Bentley?'

Miss Bentley seemed to hesitate uncomfortably before answering. With a curiously constricted feeling about his heart the major stared ahead across the lake, waiting for what she had to say.

'Two days after you,' Miss Bentley said. 'Sunday.'

'Well, make the most of them,' Signor Bompiani called.

The major felt himself sharply catch his breath, but whether in relief or astonishment or from the sudden chill of the air he never knew. Half an hour later the two cars, descending rapidly, were down in the warmth, among the still-blooming oleanders, of the lakeside.

Two mornings later Miss Bentley sat on the terrace, staring at a boiled egg. She could not think what had caused her to order a boiled egg for breakfast and she was just thinking that, after all, she did not want it very much when the major appeared.

'Do you mind if I join you?' he said. 'Is that a boiled egg you've got?'

'I thought I'd order one.'

'I think I might order one myself.'

The major rang a bell on one of the trellis posts along the terrace and, when Enrico came, ordered a boiled egg.

'Four minutes,' he said.

It was, it seemed to him, the longest four minutes of his life. Like Miss Bentley he did not know what prompted him to order the boiled egg and he knew, some time before it came, that he did not want it very much either. A recollection of Pallanza, Miss Beaumont's sarcasm about his tricks, the strange moments when he had stared at Miss Bentley at the picnic and above all the fact that Miss Bentley was going away next morning made him something more than tongue-tied and uneasy. He felt a little sick too.

'Do start,' he said. 'Don't wait. Mine is sure to be some time.'

Miss Bentley picked up a knife and prepared to slice the top off her egg. The morning sun drew from the knife blade a flick of silver light as, almost at once, she laid it down again.

The major, not daring to ask her what her plans were for her last day by the lake, raised his face to the sun and said:

'The sun's really quite warm when you think it's nearly November.'

'Yes, it's quite warm.'

'It's really been quite exceptionally warm all the month.'

'Exceptionally warm,' she said. 'Even the Italians say it's been exceptionally warm.'

Presently the egg arrived and the major found himself staring at it, unable to attack it, exactly as Miss Bentley had done.

'It seems awfully quiet without the Bompianis,' he said.

She looked away at the lake. 'Yes,' she said.

'They were so gay.'

'I suppose they were. The children got on your nerves sometimes.'

'Oh! did they? I never noticed that.'

Miss Bentley looked from the lake to her egg and then back to the lake again. As she did so the major remembered the morning, almost a month before, when she had said good-bye to him, checked his hotel bill for him and had talked to him, with such efficient assurance, about the necessity of not packing his passport and ticket with his luggage. Then she had kept her eyes fixed on the side of his face and it was he who was nervous. Now she simply stared at the egg and the lake and could not look at him.

He tapped at the top of his egg with a spoon.

'I thought –'

'What are –'

The major stopped tapping the egg.

'I'm sorry. Please –'

'It's nothing,' Miss Bentley said, 'I was only going to say

– I mean you're up rather early. Are you having a swim today?'

'No. As a matter of fact,' the major said, 'I was thinking of going up to the mountains.'

'By funicular?'

'No. You can get a bus to that village – the one where the level crossing is – and then walk from there.'

'It's quicker by funicular.'

A sudden impression that the egg might not be very fresh caused him to feel a wave of nausea. It caught in his throat. He swallowed, pushed the egg away and found himself saying:

'I suppose you wouldn't care to come? We could probably get a bite at the village and a glass of wine.'

'I really ought to do my packing.'

'It really won't take all that long,' the major said. 'I plan to be back by three.'

She made another meaningless gesture with the knife, picking it up as if to attack the egg and then putting it down again.

'I simply must do my packing,' she said.

Another pointless gesture with the knife irritated him.

'You've got hours,' he said. 'What time does your train go tomorrow?'

'That's another thing,' she said. 'I've got to get my sleeper ticket fixed. I've only an open one at the moment. I ought to have done it before –'

'Perhaps you'd rather say good-bye to Pallanza?' he said. 'I'll go to Locarno for the day.'

The jolt of pain across her face was quick and shocked, but it followed him down the hill. Walking quickly towards the lake, angry, almost marching, he suddenly hoped he would never see Miss Bentley again. His embittered remark about Pallanza was a fitting end to something that, even before the pantomime of the eggs, had begun to swell with prickly irritations. That was the way with women. You offered, you cajoled, you were reasonable, you were generous and suddenly for no reason they took flight and hid themselves away.

He decided suddenly he was in time to catch the ten o'clock steamer, make the trip up the lake, spend the day in Locarno and come back late by train. By that time Miss Bentley would have gone to bed. In the morning he would order his breakfast upstairs, read for a couple of hours and not come down till lunch time. By twelve-thirty Miss Bentley would be gone. He would have seen the last of her.

Then suddenly he was thinking 'Why the devil should I? Why, when I don't want to? Why go to Locarno when what you really want to do is to go to the mountains? Why be bludgeoned by Miss Bentley?'

He turned away from the lake and was just in time to catch a bus, in which he got a back window-seat, at the *piazza*. It took him, with many stops, up the long valley where groups of workers, some of them women still in big rice-straw sun-hats, were still gathering grapes among the vines. Over everything hung a light dust-coloured haze. The sun was hot on the windows of the bus and at one of the stops he looked out to see a hatless young Italian girl, arrogant, strong and brown as mahogany, taking off her woollen jumper among the vines. As she crossed her hands and seized the tips of the jumper and pulled it over her head she revealed underneath it the high line of her breasts, updrawn, in a white sleeveless blouse.

She laughed openly as she saw him looking at her. Then she hung the jumper over the vines and, still looking at him and still laughing, made as if to pull off the blouse too. He smiled back at her as the bus drove away and she suddenly plucked a bunch of grapes and pretended to throw it after him, following him with roving, arrogant eyes.

As the bus travelled away from the vineyards he half-wished he had got out, stopped and spent the day there. That would have been a great way to spend a day. He had always wanted to help with the vines. That would have been quite a Bacchanalian revel there, he thought, in the hot sun, in the alley-ways of vines, among the piled skips of grapes, with the brown arrogant girls.

By the time he got off the bus it was twelve o'clock. He was quite hungry and he had forgotten the look, on Miss Bentley's face, of arid, fleeting pain.

At the foot of the narrow road to the mountains stood a caffè where, on his first visit with the Bompianis and Miss Bentley, children had arrived, selling flowers. He sat at a table outside and waited. Beyond an open door screened by a curtain of coloured beads he could hear the family having lunch. He listened for some time to the murmur of voices and the sharp sounds of knives and forks and then pressed a bell in the wall.

A girl in a white sleeveless dress came, wiping food from her mouth with the corner of her apron.

'You speak English?'

'Little, little,' she said.

She smiled as she spoke. He noticed her very slim, long fingers, almost as straight as wheat stalks and the same yellowish-tawny colour. Dark hair grew thick in her neck and under her arms and her feet were bare.

'Bring me a half bottle of *orvieto*,' he said. 'And some cheese.'

'Bread with the cheese?'

She smiled again as she spoke. It was a very pleasant smile, he thought, not so bold, ripe and ready as the smile of the girl in the vineyard, but still a wonderfully pleasant, easy smile.

He responded by smiling too. She was eighteen or nineteen, he thought, though you could never tell in the south. Perhaps she was younger. 'Yes, bread, please,' he said and he watched the swing of her bare legs as she moved away.

When she came with the wine she smiled again, staying at the same time to talk a little and not only to uncork the wine but to pour it out for him; and once again he could not help thinking that the smile, like the smile of the girl in the vineyard, was specially, exclusively and solely for him. Wonderful, he thought, to drowse away the whole afternoon there, repeating the wine and the smiles until the bus came back.

'Very beautiful here,' he said. '*Molto bella*. In the mountains.'

'In the town is better.'

'You think it's better in the town? Not in the mountains? Why?'

She shrugged her shoulders slightly and with one long finger drew indeterminate patterns with a drop or two of spilled wine across the table-top.

'In the town more fun.'

'Oh! you know the word fun, do you?' he said.

'Yes, I know it,' she said. The corners of her mouth sprang up, quick and pretty. 'You think I shouldn't know?'

They responded quickly, he thought. Bathed in a glow of pleasure, the wine cold and fresh in his mouth, he sat for an hour alone, gazing at the mountains. Nobody else was eating or drinking and in the house the noises of the family gradually quietened down.

When he finally rang for the bill and the girl came he delayed her by searching in the wrong pocket for his money and then by producing a note for five thousand lire, hoping she had no change. But she had change and he sat in fascination as she counted the notes out for him on the table, his veins racing with pleasure and satisfaction as he followed the line of her bare arms to the shoulders, until finally he ran his fingers down her arm and pressed a note in her hand.

'*Basta! Basta!*' she said. She swung round in a flare of fury, pointing to the mountains. '*Basta!*' He thought she would either strike him or spit at him before she found her English again. 'We sell wine and food here! Not *me*!'

She actually did spit as, a moment later, she turned and swung into the house again. He picked up his change and started away up the road, but a rattle of curtain beads made him turn suddenly and he saw the girl appear again, this time with another, older girl, perhaps her sister, and from the beads they mocked him.

'*Papa!*' the elder one shouted. She stuck out her tongue. '*Papa!*'

He walked frigidly up the mountainside, among the rocks. He suddenly felt completely stripped. He felt he would hear for the rest of his life the jeers of the two girls from behind the curtains.

He climbed up to where the spring broke from the rocks. It was farther up than he thought and the spring itself, bursting from a wall of rock, came out faster than he remembered. Instinctively he held his hand under the descending water and the shock of it, pure ice, fell like a lock on his pulse, making him gasp for breath.

For a long time he sat listening to the water. There was nothing in it now that soothed him. It cut down into the tendons of his pride as harshly as the water itself had locked its ice on his wrist. It seemed to expose skin after skin of folly: his incredible folly about Miss Beaumont, his utter folly about the stupid, pompous tricks.

He remembered Miss Bentley. He had been, above all, an impertinent, impossible fool about Miss Bentley. With ruthlessness he had thrown at her his trite and embittered taunt about Pallanza and had fled the instant she stared at him with pain.

He started to walk back down the slope. It had been more than an hour since he had first walked up. The sun was moving rapidly westward. Already, across the fields of rock, there were big purple flanks of shadow.

Where the picnics had taken place, on a circular ledge of exposed burnt grass, the sun still shone.

He stopped suddenly at the edge of this grass and stared. In the centre of it, more or less exactly where she had lain at the picnic, Miss Bentley lay in the sun, arms outstretched, eyes closed.

He sat down. With compressed astonishment Miss Bentley opened her eyes and looked at him.

'You said you were going to Locarno.'

He searched for something to say in answer. A recollection of the blistering taunt from behind the curtain of the little caffè shot through him and kept him silent instead. Then he remembered his own impossible taunt about Pallanza and suddenly, for the first time, he felt he began to understand her pain.

'What made you come up here?' he said.

'I came to listen to the spring.'

A further recollection of the stupid evening of his tricks made him realize, for the first time too, why she had written her words about the spring. Then he was sure, suddenly, and also for the first time, that the complications about her, about himself, about everything, were slipping away.

'I'm glad you came up,' he said.

He thought he saw on her face a look of inexpressible gratitude for this remark and suddenly he bent down and kissed her.

When it was over she lay, with the faintest of smiles, looking up at him.

'That was a nice impulse,' she said. 'Even better than the one you had when you missed the train.'

'You told me to stay until a new one struck me,' he said. 'Do you remember?'

Miss Bentley found herself looking, as she had so often done, at the major's ears, that were so like small tight pink roses. She actually lifted her hand and touched one of them with the tips of her fingers. A moment later she felt an impulse of her own: an impulse to tell the major not only what his ears looked like but to confess that she too had been a fool and had never been to Pallanza.

Instead she checked herself. She was quiet and she stared at the sky. There were many ways of pursuing happiness and perhaps half of them were stupid. Most of the time you were a fool and the rest of it in pain.

The major, she decided, need never know about Pallanza. She merely smiled up at him and said:

'Such a nice impulse that I hope you'll be struck by it again.'

'I might,' he said. 'On condition.'

The major laughed for the first time, looking down into Miss Bentley's clear brown eyes.

'Tell me the joke about Miss Beaumont,' he said. 'That day at the cubicle. You remember.'

Miss Bentley began laughing too.

'It wouldn't be fair on Miss Beaumont.'

'Miss Beaumont has gone,' the major said. 'Damn Miss Beaumont.'

Miss Bentley laughed again, gaily this time, with growing excitement, and then calmed herself.

'All right,' she said. 'Come nearer. How can I possibly tell you if you sit up there?'

Laughing again, she pulled the face of the major down to her, putting her mouth against one of his small pink ears.

'Good God,' he said. 'No.'

'You see how unobservant men really are.'

He drew slightly away from her, looking down at her body, seeing it not only as it lay there in the sunlight of afternoon but also as he had seen it, floating, unexpectedly splendid, in the lake below.

'Much depends,' he said, 'on what there is to observe.'

She laughed again. With rising excitement he felt his hands slip to her breasts. Her thoughts were suddenly a racing jumble of bright impressions that included the sky, the mountains, the oleanders by the lakeside and the lake itself, stretched like a blue glass lioness in the autumn sun.

Suddenly she stopped laughing and was quiet again, holding his hands against her.

'Listen to the water,' she said. 'To the spring. Can you hear it?'

Over the mountainside there was no sound except the sound of falling water. Listening, the major heard it, as he always did, like cold music, with all its sharp and separate flutings descending rapidly and brilliantly, exhilarating in the clear still air.

Miss Bentley listened too. She supposed she had wanted all her life to listen to that sound, but now she did not hear it as the major did.

'It's like eternity, that sound,' she said. With an amazement of joy she heard it pouring through herself. 'The sound of a spring rising in the mountains.'

A Prospect of Orchards

I

MANY years ago I belonged to a young men's club where I used to play chess, read magazines and also box quite frequently, though not very seriously, with a man named Arthur Templeton. We must have been, I think, eighteen or nineteen at the time.

Templeton was a shortish leaden-footed man with weak brown eyes whose responses were those of a duck with its legs tied. His jaw was babyish, smooth and hairless, like a pale pink egg. I had taken up boxing because once, at school, in a playful scuffle, a young ox of a farmer's son had struck me on the chest with a blow of such short-armed ferocity that I was convinced my heart had stopped beating. Soon afterwards I found a friendly ex-policeman who gave me lessons, taught me that the essential art of the game lay in footwork and in a maxim of six short words: hit, stop, jab, and get away. Presently I was practising these principles on Arthur Templeton, to whose pink hairless jaw I sent so many unresisted straight lefts that it became intolerably embarrassing – so embarrassing indeed that I presently became profoundly sorry for him and gave up boxing altogether.

The friendships of youth are so often impermanent that it is perhaps not surprising that Arthur Templeton's pale pink jaw presently faded from my life with no tremor either of interest or regret. There had been no pleasure whatsoever in boxing with Arthur Templeton, exactly as there can be no pleasure in catching over and over again the same gullible gudgeon from a brook. Arthur Templeton was what is known, popularly, as a glutton for punishment and if I had any reason to be glad about anything between us it was solely because I had decided that the punishment was not, if I could help it, coming from me.

Twenty-five years later I was travelling home on a cold April evening in a train that entered a tunnel and then emerged, some minutes later, into a bright stretch of downland dried stark white by the long drought of spring.

A dazzle of sunlight after the murk of the tunnel suddenly woke life into the eyes of the man sitting opposite me. He inclined towards me a head of pinkish baldness, half holding out his hand.

'I rather think we know each other,' he said, 'don't we?'

I hesitated; there was, for me, no hope of any clue of recognition except in the brown retiring eyes and the egg-like shaven jaw.

'Templeton. Arthur,' he said.

'Good Heavens, of course,' I said. 'We used to box together.'

It is a curious and not uncommon characteristic of rather short men that they seem, if anything, to grow shorter as time goes on. Arthur Templeton, who had entirely ignored my reference to boxing, seemed not merely to have grown shorter; he had grown baldish and fleshy, with the same superciliousness of lip that frequently goes not only with men of short build but also with very fat girls who desperately attempt to conceal, by an intensely aloof proudness of face, the pain and embarrassment of their unhappy figures.

In a strange way Arthur Templeton was not at all unlike one of those fat girls. In a supercilious, aloof, but indeterminate face the one thing about him that had never changed was the pink, egg-like, ever-inviting jaw.

He seemed, I thought, extraordinarily full of confidence too.

'Never hear anything of you,' he said. 'What are you doing nowadays?'

I told him very briefly what I was doing and I felt it did not impress him. Without comment but with a sharp uppish turn of the head he looked instead at the too-clear sky, greenish now above the setting sun, across the spring-dried hills.

'Looks like another frost.'

'Nearly full moon,' I said. 'What do you do?'

'Fruit,' he said. 'Apples.'

In a fruit-growing district there is hardly anything less exciting than a meeting with yet another man who grows apples. But he went on quickly, a moment later:

'Got them on a new system,' and then added, again with that supercilious turn of the head, 'or it will be when I'm ready. I'm not ready yet.'

'What sort of system?'

'I'm developing an entirely new kind of apple.'

I did not comment on this. As I grow older I grow more and more convinced that there are two things the world does not need and can long do without. One is a blue rose; the other is an entirely new kind of apple. There are some limits, I feel, to an interference with established nature.

The train, at this moment, rushed past an orchard of apple-trees, the white smoke whirling and ducking among the black, pink-knotted arms of blossom. I stared at the smoke fading against the setting sun, the low clouds almost the colour of the still unshorn sheep grazing under the boughs, and then Arthur Templeton said:

'I don't mean *that* kind of apple.' He pointed with a gesture of contempt at the pink aisles of blossom. He seemed to sense, I thought, something of my distrust, if not my scepticism, about an interference with nature. 'I don't mean that kind of thing. That's muck.'

The apple trees looked, I thought, very beautiful, very delicate in the setting sun, the pink of the half-opened buds strange and sharp against the pale green cooling sky.

'You can produce that stuff by the ton,' he said. 'Anybody can produce that muck. No, what I mean – '

If I was abruptly arrested into looking at him quickly it was mainly because his voice had become raised. It suddenly squeaked at me.

'No, what I mean' – he thrust out his pinkish egg-like jaw and I was startled into a half-remorseful recollection of how easily and how often he had presented it to me in just that same way, many years before – 'is something absolutely new.'

Scepticism, like a troublesome eyelash, is sometimes difficult to remove from the eye in a matter of seconds and his brown eyes became aggressive, quite fork-like, as they tried to remove the doubt from my own.

'You probably don't believe me but I've very nearly got it,' he said. 'An apple that tastes like a pear – in fact has all the characteristics of a pear but remains a true apple just the same.'

Mankind delights in an abundance of useless follies. Not the least of these is the evolution of fruits which take on strange flavours to which they are not entitled, still less suited, and which nobody wants anyway. Perhaps the light of scepticism still glowed in my eye.

'You don't believe it's possible?' he said.

'Oh! anything's possible,' I said. 'After all there's a strawberry grape – '

'Not the same thing,' he snapped. 'Not the same thing at all.'

'And isn't there a pea-bean?'

'Entirely different again. Absolutely different. Not the same at all.'

'I've even heard of mint flavoured with pineapple – '

With eyes shining brown, unsuspicious, resolved and deadly serious, he looked at me with withering calm.

'You probably haven't gone into this sort of thing very much.'

'I can't say I have.'

'Ever hear of a man named Professor Kurt Schumann?'

'No.'

'California,' he said. 'He's been working on the same lines

for years. Published several papers. Oh! you can read them. They're interesting. But I believe – '

He broke off the sentence. At this point of the railway line there is a long curve at the end of the gradient where trains begin to brake very hard before running into the next station. As the brakes now went on the train jolted roughly and I thought the jerking movement gave to his apparently confident, supercilious face, taken unawares a surprising touch of innocence. He looked suddenly insecure.

A moment later, as when he had so often, in the past, offered the pink egg-like jaw for me to hit, I felt intolerably and inexplicably sorry for him.

'Well, this is my stop,' he said. 'Do you often come down by this train?'

'Fairly often.'

'Why don't you hop off and see us some time?' he said. 'You could quite easily catch the next one down. We're five minutes up the road, that's all. You could see the orchards and the whole place and I'd show you a bit of what I'm doing. We've got quite a nice place up there. Still developing of course – '

The train was stopping. He seemed about to give me a limp, podgy hand. Abruptly he changed his mind, putting on his small green homburg hat instead. For some reason the hat made him look shorter than ever. It had a green cord round the brim. It was not unlike the kind of hat you sometimes see men wearing in the Alpine villages of Austria. It had a small pink and blue feather in one side.

'Well, what about it?' he said. 'Any day.'

I have often discovered that people on trains who impulsively invite you to visit their homes next time you are passing are almost always considerably surprised and embarrassed when you take them at their word.

'Well – '

'Give us a tinkle,' he said. 'If I'm not there my wife will be.'

As I murmured the faint whispers of half-promises the train

stopped. He got out. From the platform he said 'Good-bye. See you anon, perhaps,' and lifted his still apparently supercilious face towards the smoky head of the train.

A few moments later, as the train drew out, I watched him walking, duck-footed, through the ticket barrier, podgy face thrust forward, the chin round, pink and protuberant, almost as if inviting some kind of punishment from the frosting sky.

2

It is more than likely that Arthur Templeton might have faded with insignificance from my life for a second time if it had not been that, two evenings later, my telephone rang and a woman's voice, piercing as a drill, asked if it could speak to me.

'Speaking,' I said.

'Oh! hullo,' she said. 'It's Valerie.'

I could not recall, at that moment, any woman by the name of Valerie.

'Valerie Templeton. Arthur's wife,' she said. 'Hullo, are you there?'

'Yes, I'm here.'

'Oh! good, I thought you'd gone. Did I surprise you?'

She had surprised me, though I didn't confess it.

'I wondered if I would,' she said. 'Don't you remember me?'

I did not remember her.

'That's partly Arthur's fault for not telling you,' she said. 'But then he wouldn't. Hopeless to expect it. You know Arthur, don't you?'

The fact that I knew neither Arthur nor his wife kept me locked in puzzled silence again.

This silence was presently broken by a fluffy giggle, less piercing but more forbidding than the speaking voice itself, that seemed to me like a nervous attempt to be something more than friendly.

'I believe you're kidding. You're putting it all on,' she said. 'You mean you don't remember the Pendlebury sisters?'

In a flash, across twenty-five years of time, I remembered the three Pendlebury sisters. They were fair-haired and very plump. They had faces like damp white cushions.

'Of course,' I said. 'Of course.'

'Well, I'm Valerie,' she said. 'The musical one. Have you got me now?'

I had got her now, but the fact did nothing but keep me silent again.

'Aren't you rather musical too?' she said.

'I'm very fond of music.'

'Well, that's what I really rang about,' she said. 'We know quite a few musical people here. Quite a circle of us. Not a lot of course – there aren't a lot, are there? You know what I mean? Well, not when you're stuck in the country anyway.'

I had not time to think what she meant before she went on:

'Would you like to drop in one evening on your way down from town? Arthur said you might. We sometimes have concerts.'

'Yes, he asked me,' I said. 'He wanted me to drop in and look at the experiments.'

'The what?'

The voice pierced my ear-drums so effectively that I was glad to use it as an excuse that I hadn't heard.

'He wanted me to look at the farm and – '

'What about Tuesday?' she said. 'If you came down on the five-fifteen?'

I said something about not being quite sure about Tuesday.

'Well, try,' she said. 'I'm dying to renew old acquaintance.' The fluffy, intimate giggle tripped about my ear for the second time. 'Any time. Just drop in. It would be awfully nice. No ceremony at all. Open house and that sort of thing.'

The following Tuesday evening, as I left the train and walked along the side of the valley towards Arthur Templeton's house, it seemed that every branch of every orchard was in blossom. It was very warm for April and under a white-blue sky blackbirds were singing with choking, thrilling richness among miles of pink and snowy boughs. There are springs of accidental perfection when, for a few days, all the blossom of all the orchards meets, cherry and apple and plum and pear, like a great lacy gathering of cloud; and this was one of them.

Foolishly I had neglected to ask the name of the Templeton house and when I stopped at the first neat, well-ordered farm standing at the fringe of a wide apron of blossoming cherries a heathery tweed-coated man came out of a barn to tell me, rather testily, I thought:

'Next one up the road. Can't miss it. One with the gas-tarred barn.'

Unlike Housman I am not sure which is the loveliest of trees; and as I walked up the road, between black-boughed cherries on one side and the pink up-curled horns of apple branches on the other, I felt as much impressed by the orderliness in everything, by the strict-pruned sentinels everywhere lined up in the April evening sun, as I did by the clouds of gathered blossom folded into every corner of the little valley.

Then I came, suddenly, on the gas-tarred barn. It had something of the appearance of a battered black saucepan with a makeshift lid of corrugated iron, three parts rusty, that had been tossed on top of it by a fluky throw. Some parts of it hung perilously over the western eave ready to fall. Below it a pile of rock, half-hidden by rising nettles, had wrecked a wooden trailer, turning it upside down, revealing a hole in its belly through which, presently, the nettles too would grow.

Beyond all this was the house. It struck me as being rather like a ship stranded on a muddy shore. Its upper structure, of thin weather-board, was flaky white; the Plimsoll line of red lower brick actually had in it two round portholes of thick green glass on either side of a half-glass door.

Up one wall of the house grew a vast espalier pear-tree that in its pruned stiffness was exactly like some compound arrangement of ladders for scaling the side of a ship. It was the only orderly thing in sight. All along its black, scaly branches there was not a single spray of flower.

When there was no answer to my third ring at the doorbell I started to wander about the farmyard. I had in mind to look for the seat of Arthur Templeton's experiments, for the system, well-ordered but revolutionary, by which apples would be married to pears and in time produce a sweeter, different progeny, but warm odours low on the April air led me to an arrangement of pigsties, hideous as concrete pill-boxes left over from an abandoned war, ranged between a duck pond and a clump of elder trees.

Two pale pink sows stood up to their shoulders in dung-steeped straw and contemplated me. A few white ducks were shovelling about the mud on the banks of the pond. If they inspired in me a thought of Arthur Templeton it was not through motives of vindictiveness. I was simply wondering where he was.

Presently, glancing round at a small orchard of apples, haphazardly filled in with young plums where wind or man had removed an older tree, I caught sight, out of the corner of my eye, of a figure who did not seem to belong to this scene.

It was a big, chunky man with gingerish hair and a red bow tie, hatless, who was carrying a cello in a brown canvas case. We exchanged a silent, distant, not unhostile stare before he hurried across the concrete and, without knocking, disappeared through the front door of the house.

His arrival became the signal, two minutes later, for my own moment of recognition. Across the yard, towards the pigsties, came the hurried fluffy giggle I had heard twice or more on the telephone.

'Well, there you are! Haven't changed a bit. I'd have known you anywhere.'

This was more than I could say of Valerie Templeton.

'Didn't you ring?' She was wearing spectacles with rims of exceptionally pale golden tortoiseshell, almost the colour of honey. 'I didn't hear you. I was probably practising.'

I said I had rung; the fluffy giggle was all the answer she gave me for another twenty seconds or so, during which she held out both hands, clasping my right one.

'Nice to see you,' she said. 'Damn nice. Really damn nice. How long has it been?'

If I did not answer this question in terms of specific years it was not only because I could not remember but because I was arrested, indeed astonished, by Valerie Templeton.

With the years Arthur Templeton, who in my youth had been short, weak-eyed and full of hesitancy, had grown fattish, supercilious and seemingly full of confidence. His wife, who like her two sisters had once had a face like a white plush cushion, had lost all trace of that upholstered appearance that was all I could remember of her girlhood except her fair long hair. Now the hair was piled into tiers of little watch-spring curls above a face whose cheek bones were like pared clenched knuckles. The flesh had the shining prettiness of wax, the same unreal, doll-like air, and the blue eyes were hungry.

'I was looking for Arthur,' I said.

'Oh! you know what Arthur is,' she said. 'Vague as they make them. He's gone into the town about some pigs or something. Probably forgotten you were ever coming.'

She turned on me a deliberately fascinating smile, flashing the honey-rimmed spectacles. Her mouth and her teeth, I noticed, were rather large, and perhaps it was this that gave her giggle its fluffy but unsoothing sound.

'More than you can accuse me of,' she said. 'I've been thinking about you all day. You know – wondering.'

If I had known her better I might have thought she was trying to mock me. She lifted her head and threw it slightly backwards and the gesture, like a pulled lever, released the giggle once again.

'Well, come in anyway,' she said. 'Arthur may be years. We're just having a snifter and then we're going to try the Dvorak. You know the one I mean?' With closed mouth she hummed some bars of the piece I did not recognize. 'The Quintet,' she said. 'Tum-ti-tum-ti – you know, and then that typical Dvorak lilt – tah! – you know what I mean? Damn difficult though. Hell to play.'

The interior of the house, first in an entrance hall crowded in every corner with stained mackintoshes, muddy gum-boots, baskets and several sacks that might have held samples of Arthur Templeton's apples, and then in a long sitting room furnished in dusty brown coco-matting, with chairs and settees loose-covered in bright orange linen and piled with many pink and purple velvet cushions, had the same shabby gimcrack air as the yard outside. A big tobacco-brown pseudo baronial sideboard, littered with sheets of music, stood against one wall. A black, oddly compressed baby grand seemed to cower in the opposite corner – cower, I think, is the appropriate word, for the entire bulk of the chunky 'cello-player was sprawled weightily across it, as across a bar.

After the cello-player, who was drinking whisky, had been introduced to me as 'Sandy – he's the unlucky one because the cello part's absolute murder, but you know it, don't you?' two more people arrived. Both were carrying fiddles.

It would have been hard to detect, at first glance, whether they were men or women except for the fact that one of them sported a tender, light fawn beard. A premature baldness at the temples threw into relief the heavy side curls of his hair. The sunken washed blue eyes gave him an air of sickness over which Valerie Templeton fussed with solicitude, mothering him with giggles as she unravelled the big thick red scarf that had coiled itself about his thin neck like a scarlet python.

'Thought you two were never coming,' she said. 'Bet you dawdled in the bushes on the way, didn't you? Iris Bensted! – come clean.'

If there was the remotest chance of Iris Bensted coming clean I did not detect it. She turned on the rest of us a pair of remote dark eyes as unmoved and glistening as a cow's. Her black hair was cut monkishly, in a low fringe that, trimmed as with the aid of a basin, reached to within an inch of her thick rough brows.

The fact that she was wearing a heavy cable-stitch sweater in bright green and black loose trousers accounted for my not being able to determine, with immediate certainty, what her sex was.

'Well, drinks for everybody, Sandy,' Valerie Templeton said, 'come on. Pour out, sweetheart.'

After laboriously detaching himself from the baby grand the 'cello-player poured, in a muffled, sloppy sort of way, drinks for the rest of us and presently we were standing about the room with glasses in our hands, I in a world that had taken me slightly by surprise and in which I found myself constantly wondering, and with growing depression, where Arthur Templeton could be.

'Well, I suppose we ought to make a bash at it,' Valerie Templeton said once and I assumed this meant the music. 'Sometimes I don't know why we chose the damn Dvorak. It's stinking difficult. Maddening. Absolute hell. Do you think we're bats to take it on?' she said to me, 'do you? Or what?'

No answers, I discovered, were expected to these questions, for the simple reason that Valerie Templeton always provided them, in the shape of her fluffy nervous giggles, herself.

Twilight was almost upon us before the tuning of strings began. Outside, somewhere in the region of the orchard, a blackbird was still singing – heard, I think, by no one but my-self as I went to shut a casement window in answer to Valerie Templeton's abrupt demand:

'Somebody shut the window please. It's getting chilly.'

A second or so before shutting the casement I thought I caught sight of a light in the barn across the yard. Falling darkness was shutting out the sprinkled knots of blossom on the rows of ill-pruned apple trees and a few moments later the closing of the window shut out altogether the last, rapturous singing of the blackbird.

Turning back to the room I found Valerie Templeton switching on the light and heard her say, with a sort of half-aggrieved note of apology to me:

'Don't know if you'll be able to bear it. You see we have to play the damn thing as a quartet – haven't got a blasted viola yet. Sandy – did you see that girl? Is she coming, do you know?'

'Sunday,' Sandy said.

If the need had been for a double-bass the lugubrious mutterings of the red-bowed cello-player would have provided it as he sat, softly belching whisky, tuning his strings.

'Let's hope to God she's good,' Valerie Templeton said.

'Let's hope to God she comes,' the cello-player said, 'or else we'll have to get the cat in.'

'*You* don't play the viola, do you?' she said to me. 'Too much to hope, I suppose?'

'Too much,' I said.

I sat listening, for some forty minutes longer, to the rattling of the quintet's partly assembled skeleton. Valerie Templeton played the piano like a hen pecking at a bowl of maize. In all her hungry, crouching, spectacled actions above the cowering little grand piano there was an aggressive sinewy desperation.

At ten o'clock, my mind on the last train home, I rose to go.

'Oh! must you? Was it hell? God, I bet we've bored you.' She started pulling with nervous brittleness at the joints of her fingers, as if chastising them for being responsible for the noises I had heard. 'Pity Arthur wasn't here. You could have nattered with Arthur.'

'Where is Arthur?' I said.

'Search me,' she said. 'You know what Arthur is.'

'Perhaps experimenting,' I said.

'This is the second time I've heard about these experiments,' she said. 'What's it all about?'

'Search me,' I said.

She laughed at that, rather sharply I thought, and then, in spite of my protests, she came to the door to say good night to me. In the hall she turned on me the glittering, honey rims of her spectacles and said:

'Too much to hope you'll drop in again, I suppose? You've had a bore of an evening – honest, haven't you?'

'Not a bit,' I said. 'Fascinating.'

'Well, drop in whenever you like,' she said. 'You will, won't you?' She raised her hands in the beginnings of a flutter of invitation, smiling open-mouthed, so that for a moment I was almost sure she was about to flirt with me. I was mistaken. 'After all one's got to meet somebody now and then besides *that* crowd.' She made a gesture back towards the sitting room where all was silent now. 'One's got to *live*, hasn't one? – if you know what I mean.'

Outside, in the April darkness, the blackbird had stopped its singing. The apple boughs were invisible beyond the pond. Across the yard the only glimmer of light came in a few yellow perpendicular pencil cracks through the timbers of the gas-tarred barn.

I crossed the yard, pushed open the half-fastened door of the barn and looked inside.

Sitting on a box, in the light of a hurricane lamp, crouching over a bed of straw on which stretched a shadowy figure I found for a moment or two difficult to identify, sat Arthur Templeton.

'There you are,' I said. 'Just going. Sorry I missed you.'

'Caught me at a bad time,' he said. 'Been running all over the place for a vet and couldn't find one.'

From among the straw came a grunt or two that reminded me for a moment of the mutterings of the cello-player. A ripple of pink-white legs against a barrel of ruckled teats solved

for me, a moment later, the brief mystery of Arthur Templeton's vigil and he said:

'Have to watch her. Not sure there isn't another one.'

At the same time he turned towards me the unresisting weak
brown eyes, no longer supercilious but remarkably placid now
in the lamplight, into which I had so often looked when we had
boxed together and which had made me so intolerably embarrassed and often so intolerably sad for him.

'Don't suppose you'll drop in again?' he said. 'Like to show
you – '

'Perhaps next week,' I said.

He was still smiling as I crept out. Outside not a whisper of
a sound broke the April night silence above the orchards, the
boughs of which grew whiter and whiter as my eyes became
accustomed to a darkness in which I walked slowly, brooding
more and more on Arthur Templeton, crouched in the lamplight, bringing pigs into the world.

3

When I next called at the Templetons' house, about a week
later, it was raining hard. Everywhere blossom was falling from
the apple trees. The valley that with its many orchards
had looked so like a delicate encampment of cloud had now
begun to look soiled and ragged under drenching evening
rain.

There is something intangibly melancholy in the first vani-
shing of spring blossom and perhaps it was this, combined with
the dry scratching of strings from the house, that made me
wish I hadn't called. In vain I looked into the gas-tarred barn
across the farm yard, hoping to see Arthur Templeton inside it,
mothering his little pigs or perhaps – an even vainer hope –
engaged in marrying the apple to the pear. All the sounds and
movements I found there came solely from the flood of water
pouring down from a roof hole on to the wheel of an ancient

haycutter and dripping from there to a rusty hip-bath half full of sprouting swedes.

I need not have worried, as it happened, about the intangible melancholy of the April evening permeating the heart of anyone but myself. I am perhaps oversensitive to the moods of earth and rain. I ought to have been prepared for the fact that there are people who eagerly grasp at the enclosing shrouds of sodden English evenings as heaven-sent excuses for romping jollity.

In the house, in fact, the Templetons were holding a party – or at least Mrs Templeton was. The sound of strings came from Iris Bensted's fiddle. She was being helped by the bearded fellow fiddle-player, now vamping at the piano. On the floor, from which the dusty coco-matting had been dragged back, several couples, including the cello-player and Valerie Templeton, in a brilliant emerald dress, were dancing.

'Ah! there you are!' Seeing me, she disengaged herself from the embraces of the cello-player and came tripping across the floor, locking and unlocking nervous welcoming fingers. 'You see, I told you it was a surprise, didn't I?'

This remark referred to a telephone conversation of the previous day in which she had urged on me the necessity of being an absolute dear and dropping in on them – 'because it's going to be a surprise, dear, and I think you'll like it.'

'It's my birthday!' she now said to me. 'And there's me and my candles!'

With gay imprecision she flung her arms about the air, directing my glance to the baronial sideboard, on which stood an iced birthday cake of astounding appearance which I thought for a moment had actually been made of painted cardboard.

'Do you like it? or do you think it's *terrible*?'

Gazing at this strange object, the cake, I did not know what to say. The icing had been coloured a livid vitriolic blue. Round it were set, in a double arc, numbers of bright magenta candles.

I was saved from making any comment on this by Valerie Templeton's hand suddenly clutching at my sleeve.

'You're wringing wet!' she said. 'You walked up in the rain. Where was your overcoat?'

'It was fine when I left for town this morning –'

'You'd better come upstairs and dry off or you'll catch your death or something. Your hair's all wet too. Silly man. Look at your hair.'

I started to say something about the difficulties of looking at your own hair but in her adamant, challenging, desperate fashion she seized my arm and led me away.

Upstairs we spent ten ruffled, uncomfortable, conflicting minutes in the bathroom.

'Rub your hair hard with this warm towel. I'll dry your jacket. It's not through to your shoulders, is it?'

I begged her several times not to fuss with me but she took no notice and presently she insisted I took my jacket off. After this she ran her hands over the shoulders of my shirt, then over the cuffs and the collar.

Presently, still towelling my hair, I stood facing her.

'You look funny with your hair all ruffled,' she said.

'Naturally.'

I was annoyed; I spoke acidly and she smiled at me.

'I mean funny nice.'

'Whatever that may mean.'

She laughed again, not quite so fluffily as she did sometimes, but in a lower voice, more smoothly.

'I hoped it might mean you'd give me a birthday kiss.'

'What gave you that idea?'

'You're funny. You're awfully nice,' she said. 'You always were.'

The retreat from kisses he does not want is one of the unpleasantest things that can happen to a man. I began to be angry.

'Do your eyes always go that bright blue colour when you're angry?' she said.

'I'm not angry,' I said. 'Nor is my head quite so wet as you think it is.'

'That was good. You were always quick-witted.'

I started savagely to comb my hair. She laughed and tried to take the comb away.

'Kiss me,' she said. 'Come on, kiss me.'

'Now look, let's get downstairs –'

'Kiss me,' she said and it was hard to tell whether her voice was wild or miserable, or, like her eyes, simply desperate with hunger. 'Come on, be a sport. Kiss me. Just once. Be a sport. Show me how you –'

What followed was so impossibly absurd that I can only describe it, if the simile is not too ridiculous, as trying to avoid being caressed by a mule that is at the same time frantically struggling to kick over the traces. We rocked, stupid and dishevelled, about the bathroom. She aimed a whole volley of vindictively amorous kisses at my face and laughed unflinchingly, showing a quivering crimson tongue.

'Be a sport. My God,' she kept saying, 'you and me could have fun.'

'Have fun with Arthur!' I said.

It was suddenly as if I had translated into action precisely what I had in mind to do to her. If I had suddenly held her silly face under the cold bath-tap I could not have shocked her more completely to her senses.

'My God, my God, Arthur,' she said. 'Arthur! – Arthur!'

She stood looking at me with a mixture of pity, contempt, misery – all sorts of things. She even laughed again. The vindictively amorous hunger faded in a second, completely.

'Better get back to the party,' she said.

She picked up my jacket from the floor and gave it back to me.

I put it on. 'Now you're talking sense,' I said. 'Why didn't you say that before?'

She didn't answer. I brushed my hand across the damp lapels of my jacket and buttoned it up.

'Damn it,' I said. 'Arthur's a good sort.'

From behind the honey rims of the spectacles she stood looking at me in a final moment of supremely miserable, withering calm.

'Good sort?' she said. 'Good sort? – that's what the road to hell's paved with! – good sorts.'

We had scarcely been downstairs for a quarter of a minute before we were confronted by a dutiful Arthur Templeton, the good sort, holding an empty tray.

'Drink?'

Before I could answer his question she was rasping at him:

'Of course he wants a drink! Don't be woolly. What the hell do you think he wants? – the evening paper or something? What's the use of prancing about with an empty tray?'

He took this searing punishment like a lamb.

'Gin, whisky or a glass of red wine?'

'Glass of wine, Arthur, thanks,' I said.

To my surprise, as Arthur retreated, she became her old giggling self again.

'I *knew* you were a red wine man,' she said. 'You can see it in your eye.'

A minute later, Arthur Templeton came back, bearing a glass of cold red wine in his hand.

'Oh! grip, Arthur, grip!' she said. 'First the tray without the glass. Now the glass without the tray!'

'Sorry,' Arthur said to me and held out not only the glass but that smooth inviting jaw, supercilious no longer, which I had struck so often many years before.

'I wanted something different,' she said. It was lost on me for a moment, as I watched Arthur Templeton retreating, duck-footed, among the dancers, that she was referring yet again to the cake on the sideboard. 'I get so tired of white, don't you?

127

Everybody gets so stuck in awful ruts, don't they? Don't you always think it looks like a starched shirt front, that white icing – so terribly chapel-and-church?'

I was about to admit that there was some truth in this when she waved her indecisive hands again, giggling with a voice that flapped featherily, and said:

'You know a few people, don't you? You don't want to be introduced all over the place, do you? We don't want to be formal, do we? If you get stuck with anybody ghastly make signals and I'll come and rescue.'

'I'll probably talk to Arthur,' I said.

'God, that's a prospect,' she said. From behind her honey rims she darted arrowing glances about the room and its crowd of dancers, as if seeking someone who would save me from this fate. 'Oh! I know – you haven't met the kid yet. The viola player. That's her – over there, talking to Sandy.'

A girl of perhaps nineteen or twenty, pretty, fair-haired, with a golden plum-like skin, looking not at all unlike the Valerie Templeton I remembered from the years when I boxed with Arthur, stood leaning against the far wall, talking to the cello-player.

'She isn't bad,' Valerie Templeton said. 'She's a pupil of Sandy's – of course he couldn't teach pussy, but the poor devil's got to live, I suppose. Come on, let's drag him away – he's breathing all over her.'

She needed no assistance, I noticed, in dragging the cello-player away.

'Come on, you coarse brute,' she said playfully. 'Come and dance with me.'

In an atmosphere of stringy pandemonium I talked, for the next fifteen or twenty minutes, to the girl who played the viola. Anthea Barlow was her name. I had not been mistaken in thinking that on her fair soft skin there was a downy plum-like bloom. Her eyes too had a surface of tenderest limpidity through which the pupils shone with disarming brilliance – innocent as forget-me-nots, or so it seemed to me.

As I struggled to make small conversation about music she turned these eyes on me with continually mounting surprise.

'Oh! really,' she would say. 'Do you think so? I never thought of that. Isn't that interesting?'

I had just begun to think of making the necessary signals to Valerie Templeton when Arthur arrived.

'Gin, whisky or red wine?'

His simple catechism having been repeated, he stood back, staring at the girl, his hands twisting at his empty tray.

'Well, I don't really know,' the girl began to say and then hesitated, turning on him the eyes of forget-me-not innocence, as if in appeal.

'Do you think I might have orange?'

'Orange,' he said, 'of course. At least I think so.'

'Is it an awful trouble?'

'Oh! no,' he said. 'Oh! no. Fresh orange or bottle? No trouble.'

'Would there be fresh?' she said.

'Oh! I'm sure there is,' he said. 'I'm sure – certain there must be.'

He retreated, face still towards us for some paces, as I remembered him so often retreating across the canvas of the boxing ring many years before.

'Are you sure it isn't an awful bother?' she called after him.

He simply went, not answering. It could not conceivably have been his first meeting with her or his first glance into those almost too blue, too innocent eyes of disarming tenderness, but I thought I caught in his retreating, suddenly suffocated eyes a look of stupefaction.

He was back in five minutes, eager as a lackey expecting a tip, bearing a long glass of crushed fresh orange juice, a basin of sugar and several straws on a tray.

'Hope I haven't been too long,' he said.

There was no suggestion of pity in her long, smiling glance at him. Nor did her eyes turn on him with that wide and mounting surprise she had exercised on me. I could see, instead, that she was greatly flattered by what she saw.

'Something else I can get you?' he said. 'There are some quite decent sandwiches. *Foie gras*, I think. Shall I go and see? Or would you rather have ham?'

'Would it be an awful – '

He went like a shot, not waiting for an answer. With blue eyes downcast and seemingly more than ever innocent, she sucked at orange juice through a pair of straws. An uncomfortable suspicion that she did not know what *foie gras* was entered my mind and leapt out again, still more uncomfortably, an instant later. And it was like a mere mocking echo of it when I heard him say:

'Terribly sorry. They weren't *foie gras*. They're smoked *trout pâté*. I brought some along – '

'Oh! Do you mind after all?' she said, 'I'd really rather have ham.'

He had hardly finished the third of these dutiful errands for her when the shrill voice of Valerie Templeton began urgently calling him, piercing as a drill above the dance music, to attend to one of her own. He obeyed that call too with his strange, unhesitant, duck-footed alacrity.

When he had retreated again the forget-me-not eyes turned themselves on me as transparent as beads of glass.

'He's a lamb.'

It might have been not inappropriate, I thought, if she'd called him a dog.

'Have you known him long?'

'No,' I said.

'I had an idea you knew him quite well.'

'Hardly at all,' I said.

'Oh! really,' she said. 'How interesting.'

The evening offered no opportunity to know him better –

except for one swift and tiny incident the significance of which, an hour later, very nearly escaped me.

'Cake being cut! Cake being cut!' I heard several voices call. 'Matches, somebody! Candles!'

This time, oppressed by the growing warmth of a room stuffy with dancers, I had gone to open a window, not to close one. To my surprise the rain had stopped. In a calm, cuckoo-less April darkness only the last drippings of a leaking gutter and the running of a ditch somewhere over against the pond broke the silence below a sky pricked with almost frosty stars.

I turned from this scene of fresh and scintillating air to see a handful of flame rising like the burners of a blue gas-ring in the middle of the baronial sideboard. Somebody had switched the electric lights out and Valerie Templeton's birthday candles were all the illumination – their flames pretty as crocuses on slender magenta stems – that now broke the darkness of the room.

'One good puff!' somebody was shouting. 'Deep breath! Now! – '

A fluffy hurricane, part giggle, part expiration, swept about the candle flames, making them flutter sideways like golden flags. About half of Valerie Templeton's forty-five years were extinguished in a single second. The rest rallied, uprighted themselves and burned unquenchably on.

The beginning of a witty quip about a woman's age was drowned in sudden laughter. The lights went up. A few moments later Valerie Templeton, over-flushed, her indecisive hands held steady by the hairy paw of the cello-player, was cutting into the blue crust of the birthday cake, among the ring of half-black, half-flaming candles.

'Happy birthday!' several people shouted. There were waves of laughter. 'Jolly good luck! – '

The knife made a sudden slip against the side of the cake's blue and brittle decorations and in laughing disgust Valerie

Templeton threw it on the sideboard, uplifting at the same time a pair of tipsy arms that the cello-player a moment later folded to his shoulders, on which she in turn laid a head of golden watch-spring curls, slightly ruffled, to be borne away to dancing.

Among all these incidents not one surprised me. It was only some ten or fifteen minutes later, when every guest had toyed or was toying with a segment of blue-edged birthday cake, that I looked across the room to see Arthur Templeton engaged on yet another errand of mercy, carrying a plate of cake to Anthea Barlow, the viola-player, still standing apart in the corner of the room.

I was too far away, in that moment, to hear what comment she offered as Arthur Templeton stood before her, like a servant placing a long-awaited offering under a pair of too bright eyes, but I could see that she hesitated.

He greeted this hesitation with an eager outward thrust of the jaw. I saw her mouth move in return, first with words, then with the fraction of a smile, and a moment later he was on the run again, bearing the plate away.

Half a minute later I pressed my way among the dancers and past the sideboard. With bent head Arthur Templeton was engaged in an absorbed meticulous task there, a knife in his hand.

In the light of two or three of Valerie Templeton's still remaining, still burning candles he was engaged in paring from a wedge of birthday cake, as from a piece of cheese, every vestige of blue icing.

And as I turned away I saw in the corner the waiting figure of Anthea Barlow, both hands slightly upraised in front of her body – for all the world as if she was about to clap them and bring him running.

4

I suppose I went to that house again three or four times, perhaps even five or six, before I finally grasped about Arthur Templeton a conclusion I ought to have reached not less than twenty years before. It was not until a burning, breathless evening in August – there had been no drop of rain since June and now in the farmyard the dregs of the never handsome duck-pond had dried to a black-green crust that sprouted a crop of skeleton elder-boughs and rusted tins – that I realized how abysmally, intolerably lonely he was. I had really been very obtuse; even the little pigs should have made it clear to me.

When I arrived that evening he was standing, shirt-sleeved, against the door post of the barn, gazing out across the yard. At the sound of my footsteps across the sun-baked track that led in from the road he jerked his body off the post and abruptly started forward – eager, as I thought, to greet me.

As soon as he saw who it was, however, he relaxed – no, relaxed is altogether too mild and indefinite a word. He flopped – exactly as if winded, punctured or worn out by heat or something – against the open door.

'Thought for a minute it was Miss Barlow,' he said. I fastened on the formal prefix to Anthea Barlow's name with a glance of inquiry at him that gave me nothing at all in answer. He was simply staring at the road. 'Her bus only gets as far as the station. She has to walk up the hill.'

Suddenly in that airless blistering evening I found myself facing the stifling prospect of Valerie Templeton's quintet, sawing its way through an August heat-wave. I half-heard, I thought, a warning echo of screaming strings on the breathless air and said quickly, a second later:

'I didn't really mean to stay. I just dropped in for a minute. If there's a rehearsal I'll just say "Hullo" to Valerie and then – '

'Oh! there's no practice,' he said. 'Valerie's taken the car down to the sea. She's rented a bungalow there. She'll be gone a night or two –'

His face became a mask, offering me no help at all. Behind and beyond him the face of the land, its light soil burnt out by weeks of sun, had become a mask too, with hardly a trace of the green that had graced it in early spring, at the time of apple bloom. A kind of brown crust, in reality the shrivelled leaves of long unwatered trees, had spread about the branches of the orchard. On the house the pear-tree was a mere trellis of blistered timber. Even elderberries were withering and falling, like shrivelled pepper-corns, from their branches above the dried-up pond. Over the western crest of the hill the sun was dropping into a shimmering sky of smoky-purple haze, burning like a deep flame above an altar.

'God, it's hot,' he said. A glaze had spread across his eyes. 'I'll get you a drink –'

'No, no,' I said. 'Don't bother –'

Almost before I had finished speaking he threw out an extraordinary remark.

'Reminds me of once when we were boxing,' he said. 'We started in September that year – the club opened about the third week – and all of a sudden we had a heat-wave.'

Not once, all that summer, had he ever mentioned the painful, long-buried episode of our boxing.

'Can't say I remember that,' I began to say.

'Oh! I do, I do,' he said. 'Perfectly. You were pretty accurate that night. I just couldn't get the measure of you –'

Here I found myself thirsting to ask him something that had perplexed me for a long long time.

'You never hit me back enough,' I said. 'You never covered up. If you'd covered up more you could have hit me more.'

'That's where I went wrong?'

'Mostly,' I said. 'You didn't hit me back enough, man. Why on earth didn't you?'

Gropingly the brown eyes searched the road beyond me.

'I suppose because I rather liked you.'

It was a remark that I found so astonishing that I could give it no answer at all. In the following silence he became jumpy again, eyes again searching the road, and he finally looked at his watch.

'Anthea must have missed her bus,' he said in a dry voice. 'I think I'll walk down to meet her. Will you wait? The house is open. Help yourself to a drink – everything's on the sideboard.'

He started to duck-paddle across the yard and then stopped so suddenly that he actually raised a skid of dust with his feet as he turned.

'I suppose you know all about us?' he said. 'I mean, Miss Barlow and me? I suppose everybody knows.'

I did not know; I was happily free of any tongues that must have been whispering among the orchards.

'I thought everybody probably knew – you know, with Valerie going away and all that. She's got this bungalow by the sea. Shares it with Sandy. You remember Sandy? It's all – '

Every trace of that protective supercilious glaze I had noted on that first sharp spring evening in the train, together with its puffed air of confidence, had left him now.

'You'll wait, won't you?' he said. 'Do wait. Don't go till I come back. Help yourself to a drink. Hang on, old man, won't you – '

With such jittery affectionate terms he crossed the yard, half-running, and went down the hill beyond.

When he had gone at last I went into the house and poured myself a long drink from the sideboard on which Valerie Templeton had extinguished some of the burning candles of her years and where Arthur had so carefully pared away for Anthea Barlow the unwanted rind of the birthday cake's harsh blue icing.

Even then it still didn't occur to me how deeply, how intolerably lonely he was.

'He's just a stupid coward,' I kept telling myself. 'That's all. A plain stupid coward. That's why he didn't hit me. That's why –'

'Anybody at home?'

My thoughts on cowardice, themselves more than a little stupid, were suddenly brought to an end by the voice of Anthea Barlow, calling through the open front door of the house from the farmyard.

'Oh! it's you,' she said when I went to the door, 'isn't Arthur? –'

'He went down the road to meet you,' I said, 'only five minutes ago.'

'I got off the bus at the other stop,' she said, 'and walked up by the foot-path. It was cooler that way – well, anyway not quite so hot.'

In the heat of the evening she looked flushed and exhausted. She received with a panting smile my suggestion that I should get her a drink and then, as I poured it out at the baronial sideboard, made one of her own.

'Let's sit outside,' she said. 'I can't bear this room. I hate that awful sideboard.'

On what ought to have been a lawn but that was now a ruckled brown mattress of untrimmed grass scorched yellow-brown by summer we sat in discoloured canvas deck-chairs, sipping drinks and gazing through the hot evening to the orchard beyond.

This was the orchard where, as I had once so fondly imagined, those great experiments of Arthur Templeton's would find their genesis and their final fruit, and perhaps she read my thoughts as we sat staring at the summer-blistered boughs, under the farthest of which I could just make out the growing litter of piglets and their sow, rooting dustily.

'Arthur's going to do a lot of new grafting in the orchard next winter,' she said.

'Oh?'

'You know the way I mean?' she said. 'You cut down the old branches and graft on different varieties.'

'Yes.'

'You know he's got this wonderful idea of a new kind of apple?' she said, 'don't you?'

There is some virtue in lying on certain occasions and I felt this was one of them.

'No,' I said.

'It's this marvellous idea of an entirely different kind of fruit,' she said, 'a cross between an apple and a pear. He's been working on it for years. There's a professor in – ' She went on with Arthur's story, in Arthur's words, and I listened, musing and dazed. The sow and her litter had been turned into the orchard, I now realized, in order to scavenge on the little prematurely ripened fruit that drought had brought down from the boughs, and they wandered gruntingly under the trees, picking up a yellow scrap or two here and there.

'Of course it'll take years,' she said. 'There's a tremendous lot of work – research and all that. But wouldn't it be marvellous?'

'Marvellous.'

'I can't help thinking of the first time you would offer a fruit like that to someone,' she said. ' "Have an apple," you'd say, and then you'd wait to see the look on their faces.'

'What look?'

'Oh! you know, the look of – the great surprise. The apple wouldn't have the taste they thought it would. You'd really catch them, wouldn't you?'

I was saved from any answer to this by the sudden voice of Arthur Templeton, whistling from the yard. It was a peculiar whistle, low, bird-like, on three abbreviated notes, and suddenly I realized it was his secret, personal call.

'That's Arthur,' she said. 'That's his whistle now.'

She jumped up from the deck chair and started running round the side of the house to the farmyard beyond. I ought to have stayed where I was, but curiosity impelled me, with my drink still in my hand, to the edge of the lawn, where a gap in a trellis-work of withered rambler roses gave me a view of the dusty square of yard.

It was then that I witnessed, at last, the exposure of his loneliness. The girl was standing with her back to me and she looked, I thought, for all the world as I remembered Valerie Templeton looking, fair, plump and soft, more than twenty years before. And suddenly I realized that he was not really looking at her. Hungrily and helplessly he stood staring at her with an adoration that was not meant for her at all.

'Because I rather liked you,' I could hear him saying to me again. 'I suppose because I rather liked you.'

A moment later I went to replace my empty glass on the baronial sideboard that Anthea Barlow hated so much. And soon I came out of the house to find her talking to Arthur at the gate of the orchard – and, to my surprise, arguing with him slightly.

'I'll say good-bye,' I said.

'Oh! before you go,' she said, 'you can settle something. Arthur and I are going for a walk. Arthur says it'll be much hotter *that* way – up the hill – and I say it'll be much hotter *that* way – down the hill. What do you think?'

'Oh! I didn't really say that,' he started to say. 'I wanted to go which way was best, that's all. Whichever way you want.'

His voice was like a broken echo. His jaw was smoothly held out, unprotected, ever-inviting.

'There's probably more breeze on the hill,' I managed to say.

'Well, of course,' she said. 'Come on, you silly man.' She turned to me with a look of triumph that was neither warm nor radiant. 'Isn't that just like him?' she said and it might have been the voice of Valerie Templeton.

I watched them walk up the slope of the hill, between the apple trees. With intensely focused light the sun was burning every moment with deeper, fiercer orange beyond the scrubby blackened apple boughs, under which the pigs were still rootling. At the crest of the slope Arthur Templeton and the girl stopped for a moment and she stooped and picked up a yellow apple and held it in her hands: an apple that might well, I thought, have been a pear.

A second later she threw it away. It needed only a call from her to set him running after it, like a dog running for a ball or like one of the pigs searching for the dropped fruits of summer; but it never came.

They disappeared at last into the sun. Above where it blazed there was not a single sacrificial fleece of cloud and there was not a breath of air to break the evening silence of all the miles of orchards about the valley until, some moments later, I heard a sound.

It was the sound of Anthea Barlow laughing. But what she was laughing at – whether it was Arthur Templeton or the little pigs or the apple that would taste like a pear or simply at some other prospect of orchards in the future – it was quite impossible to say.

The Grapes of Paradise

I FIRST caught sight of him about three o'clock in the afternoon, at the start of a humid and torrential squall of rain on the waterfront of Papeete. He was tall, lean and English to the bone, with eyes of transparent whitish blue and receding fair hair that made him look much older than he really was. The hair badly needed trimming at the neck. His shirt of pale lavender, sun-faded and worn outside his crumpled brown trousers and with a small design of darting indigo fish across it, was remarkably subdued for those parts and had not been washed for some time. It was too early to tell whether he was ill, drunk or troubled, or perhaps all three, but he was completely oblivious of the rain.

He was in fact not drunk. He had not been drunk for some considerable time. All he was doing was to watch the passage of a little motor-schooner beating shorewards through the gap of coral reef a mile or two out to sea. The flow of ocean in and out of the gap was very fast there and he kept beating his hands together like a man watching a horse-race in which he is afraid his favourite cannot win.

I watched all this through the open door of a barber's saloon. He stood quite alone on the waterfront in the rain, staring at the schooner, the breadth of the street away. Inside the reef the squall of rain became sometimes so dark that beyond it there appeared to be continuous plumes of dirty smoke where normally the vast breaking crests of spray on the collar of rocks would have shown like the rearing waves of pure white horses.

Somewhere between plumes of smoke and rain the schooner, rolling like a squat white drum, occasionally disappeared. All the time, far beyond her and the smoking reef, the Pacific flared in sunlight, a harsh clear glitter outside the storm, and beyond it all the fantastic mountains of another island glowed like half-melted pale green candles in the sky.

When the rain suddenly stopped he stood watching for nearly another ten minutes until the schooner drifted in at last and tied up below him, fifty yards away. As soon as she tied up he started to walk towards her. Then he suddenly stopped, seemed to change his mind completely and turned on his heel.

That was the first time I ever saw his face. My impression had been that he was about to meet someone off the schooner, that they hadn't arrived and that he was disappointed. Instead I saw that his eyes were extraordinarily savage: not savage with anger or the intensity of disappointment but inwardly savage, with pure blind melancholy, perhaps against himself.

That was the second impression I got: that, when he came and sat in the barber's chair next to me, hair and face and the balding reaches about his temples still streaming with rain, he was living in a state of emotional sightlessness. He picked up a towel from a wash-basin and started to rub his face and hair. His shirt was open down the front, showing a chest of pale amber hair, and he dried that too. When he had finished he lay back in the chair, shut his eyes and stretched out his arms to the wet knees of his trousers. The hands went limp, turning downwards, loosely, as if he were very tired, and as they did so I saw a scar, ten or twelve inches long, a raw brown-pink slash running from above one wrist to the muscle of the upper arm.

The barber began to comb and cut his hair without a word. Soon after he had started a girl came along the pavement outside, wheeling a bicycle. She stopped, leaned one foot against the bicycle and stared at the four men in the saloon.

'Hullo, Harry,' she said.

She spoke in good English, but he made no effort to open his eyes or answer. She was not wearing the customary *pereu* of Tahitian girls, but a sleeveless dress of pale green, with no design at all. Her hair was not plaited but was brushed in two dry black bunches, like combed rope, over her bare shoulders. She was pretty in the pert and delicate way, light and bird-like, that comes when Chinese blood is mixed with Polynesian, and her waist and legs were wonderfully fine and slender.

For another ten minutes or so, leaning on the bicycle at the open door of the saloon, she went on talking to him, saying that she hadn't seen him lately, asking if he'd seen this person or that and why did he never come dancing at the New Pacific now? All the time he neither opened his eyes nor answered.

'They tell me you're off on the next flying-boat,' she said, but even that had no effect on him.

By this time the sun was shining again and the air, delicious after the rain, was steaming hotly. The handles of the girl's bicycle glittered as she twisted them. Her hair had steel blue lights in it as she flicked it back over her shoulders and she said, for the last time:

'Well, tell me if you do, Harry. I'll come and see you off. I'll come and say good-bye.'

Impassively he ordered a massage. He seemed to know instinctively, without turning his head, that she had left. A few moments later he actually opened his eyes. All the keener edge of their savagery had now become blurred and their queer white blueness was merely glassy as he turned to me.

'English paper you're reading?'

'Yes,' I said. 'Have it if you like. You're welcome.'

'No thanks.'

'Absolutely the latest,' I said. 'Only two weeks old.'

Jokes that fail with strangers in strange places are colder than icebergs. He did not answer.

Outside the saloon the street had already steamed to concrete dryness. At the extreme end of the reef the rearing lines of sea-foam pranced with splendour in the sun. Beyond it the distant island slopes glowed with deeper, clearer green, the candle fissures almost purple in the far brilliant air.

'They tell me the other island is very beautiful,' I said.

'Not been there yet?'

'Not yet.'

'Schooner twice a week,' he said.

His voice was unexpectedly soft. The short cryptic words that ought to have made it sharp had in fact the opposite effect. He gave an impression of talking quietly to himself, meditating.

'Anywhere to stay when you get there?' I said.

'Rest-house.'

'Any good?'

'Don't know,' he said. 'Haven't seen it for a month or two. Dare say it's good. Dare say they'd fit you up.'

This, the longest piece of conversation he had offered so far, was also remarkable because during the final part of it he actually turned and gave me a glance that had in it the beginnings of a smile.

'What are you here for?' he said. 'Usual thing? Looking for the lost Loti Lotus Land or the Gauguin ghosts?'

These sentences were neither cryptic nor bitter. Nor were they exactly sarcastic or sad. The odd thing about them was their emptiness. They might have been a few spiritless puffs of air let out of a paper bag.

'I'm not sure what I've come for,' I said. 'It's like eating mangoes for the first time. You know they won't taste like oranges but what else do you expect? You don't know.'

He may have thought that this showed, perhaps, a slightly higher degree of intelligence than anything I had said before because he then said:

'That'll save you a load of disappointment. Oh! the girls are beautiful – some of them. Oh! They'll give you what you ask for.'

The barber, who had finished my hair, now gave me the towel. For a few minutes I sat reflectively rubbing my neck and face and ears. It was so hot already after the rain that my eyes were damp with sweat and my throat was parched.

'Like to join me in a drink?' I said. 'When you've finished? It's pretty hot in here.'

'I don't,' he said. 'Don't drink, I mean.'

'We could get a taxi and drive back to the hotel,' I said. 'It's cooler there.'

'I'll be ten minutes yet,' he said.

I couldn't make up my mind whether this meant he was coming or not until he said, 'I'm afraid I'm only an orange-juicer. Or passion-fruit.' He actually gave a laugh in that dry puffed way of his and again nothing, I thought, could have been more passionless.

Twenty minutes later we were driving along the waterfront, past the Postes et Télégraphe building, the last shops and the thick bright hedges of hibiscus and bignonia that flank the gardens along the black sand shore. Heat beat up in slaty glittering waves from the tarmac, sprang from waste stretches of dust under thin high palms and turned the yellow bells of creepers on fences to fleshy shimmering gold.

At the hotel he ordered, as he had promised, an orange juice. The handsomest of Tahitian girls brought it, with a glass bowl of ice and a soda siphon, on a bamboo tray.

'Nice to see you up here again, Mr Rockley,' she said. 'Soda? Have you enough ice in there?'

He made no answer. Instead he sat looking beyond the low tidal stretches of water inside the reef and then far beyond the rearing crests of the reef to where, more fantastic than ever in the more westerly angle of sun, the mountains rose like pale green candles melting but never lessening in the harsh fine air.

'Cheers,' I said.

'Good luck,' he said.

He lay back in his chair, white-blue eyes empty again and almost completely transparent, his arms flat out, the palms turned down, the fingers twitching. The scar was like a jagged brown boot-lace. And suddenly I realized that his habit of sitting with his palms downward, twitching his fingers, must have grown unconsciously out of pain.

Then he saw me looking at it. He looked surprisingly neat and respectable now, with his fresh-trimmed, fresh-massaged hair, but the barber had not been able to trim his voice or change its tone at all. It was still remarkably soft, passionless and unabrupt as he ran one finger down the scar, stared at it in silence for a moment and then said:

'Take good care nobody does that to you.'

2

He was single, unassuming, friendly and about thirty-five. He had come down to Tahiti from Vancouver, crossing the Pacific by way of Fiji, Samoa and the Cook Islands, three months before, full of conventional thoughts about romantic places.

He had in fact been overworking and had been given three months leave by the firm of industrial bankers for which he worked in Vancouver and when I talked to him that first afternoon, over his modest orange-juice, with his eyes almost always fixed on the mountains, he had already taken a month more than his time.

At first there was nothing at all unconventional in what he had to say. There is a common expression about Tahiti which is, I suppose, often made about other places but is made with more truth about this island that everyone so much expects to be a paradise. Two weeks there are too long, it says, and a year not long enough.

He had not been on the island more than a day or two before he felt convinced of the truth of the first part of the expression. When he arrived by flying boat, in the cool of a tropical evening, an hour before dusk, the waterfront was gay with a great crowd of girls in brilliant crimson *pereus*, women in pretty summer dresses, men in bright-patterned shirts, almost all of them carrying *leis* or *couronnes* of orchid, gardenia, hibiscus, jasmine and tiare flower. Most of them were shouting, laughing, throwing kisses and waving their hands; a few were weeping with joy. There were so many flowers that he felt that every garden had been stripped. The air was sweet and sickly with the scent of them.

Out of all this, as he stepped ashore, a plump Tahitian girl came forward, put her gold-brown arms on his shoulders, laughed softly and kissed him splendidly on the lips. After that she put a *lei* of frangipani round his neck and then suddenly went away to do the same service for another visitor. Then another girl put another *lei* round his neck, this time of small cherry-coloured hibiscus and jasmine, and then another girl a third. He felt slightly embarrassed by this excess of flowers, which were by now piled like Elizabethan ruffles up to his ears, but he laughed too when he saw that all of his fellow passengers were also hidden under flowers, some of them under six or seven *leis* of purple, white, orange and vermilion, some of the women wearing enchanting *couronnes*, gay little hats of purple orchid bloom.

That night at the hotel, on the edge of the lagoon, under electrically lighted coconut palms that sometimes fluttered in a wave of cool wind coming off the sea, where until long past midnight fishing boats with flares were floating about the black water, he drank champagne and did a little dancing to the three-piece orchestra of two men and a girl, who played mostly Tahitian tunes. The girl also sang songs and as time went on he thought all the songs had in them the same indescribable sadness. Two other girls, one of them not more than twelve, both bare to the navel except for a strip of covering across their breasts, did several native dances, swinging and rolling their hips, making gestures of voluptuous and graceful supplication with their light-brown hands, swishing their light skirts of hibiscus bark – not grass, as he had always imagined – dryly in the night air.

He had several dances with one or two of the women passengers from the plane and one each, out of courtesy, with the two air hostesses, pleasant girls from Adelaide. He bought a drink or two at the bar. The atmosphere had in it a great sense of careless easiness. Frenchmen danced with Tahitian girls; French women with Tahitian men.

'It was all very nice and free and easy and fresh to me,' he said, 'except that I might just as well have been in Nice or San Francisco or Paris or Sydney, though I didn't know it at the time.'

In the morning he took a taxi, drove into the town, cashed a cheque at the Bank of Indo-China and looked at the shops. The cashing of the cheque took him the better part of an hour and a half and in less than half that time he had looked at all the shops. The town had something of the air of a dusty and fly-blown French provincial town crossed with a mid-western shack-town populated mostly by Chinese. A few ancient white-painted schooners were being loaded with crates and barrels and bicycles and all manner of goods on the waterfront, where loafers sat about drinking milk out of green coconuts or bottles of fruit juice out of straws, spitting at the dust.

'It all looked so bloody fly-blown and so tatty,' he said, 'I could have vomited.'

That very morning, in fact, he went into the offices of the Pacific Navigation Company, cancelled his passage of three months hence and took a ticket on the next plane outward.

'It was as bad as that,' he said, 'and what made it worse was that nobody seemed to care a damn whether I went or stayed.'

Then he went back to the hotel, stripped off, put on his swimming trunks and went down to the sea. The beach of black sand, such as there was of it, looked like a foundry yard. The lagoon of black water illuminated by the flares of mysterious midnight fishing-boats had become a stretch of tidal junk-yard, one foot deep, filled with countless black clusters of sea-birds and lengths of what looked like yellow intestine.

At the end of fifty yards of jetty sprouted a lump of coral rock. On the rock a French girl with a figure as flat as a boy's and legs like white peeled sticks sat staring down into forty feet of dark blue water from which rose shadowy mountains of rust-brown coral, murderous as steel.

'I'm glad you came,' she said. 'If there's someone watching, the sharks don't follow me.'

He decided not to swim. Instead he went back to the bar, sat on a high bamboo stool just as he was in his swimming trunks, and dejectedly ordered himself a whisky. He sat drinking till three o'clock.

He was still drinking, but still more dejectedly, three weeks later. By that time he had toured the island twice, had eaten sucking pig several times and had not taken a single swim in the repulsive, sea-egged lagoon. The dazzling beaches of white coral of which he had heard so much and of which he had actually seen pictures on posters simply did not exist. In the shops he bought as presents a few shells of polished mother-of-pearl, a boar's tusk and a piece of native wood carving in the form of a pineapple cut in half. He sat in bars and watched dust blow out of pot-holes in the road outside and then blow back again. He drank with all sorts of people in all sorts of places and tried to laugh, above the sound of loudspeakers that might have been blaring out of any street between Sydney and Southend, at the jokes they made.

'Better take a *vahini*,' someone said, 'and settle down and get it out of your system.'

He agreed that the girls were beautiful. Their willingness in the realms of cohabitation was not simply legendary. He was fascinated with the splendid handsome readiness of their laughter. He liked above all a certain air of surface shyness in them, the grace of their walk on flat feet and the black strength of their waist-long hair.

'Anyway that's neither here nor there,' he said. 'I never saw one I really wanted. The point is that I suddenly realized that what they say is true. Two weeks are too long and a year isn't long enough. Just before the plane was due out I cancelled my ticket and booked myself on the next one. Then I did the same with that one. And at the end of the month I was – '

He stopped speaking. Since he had hardly given up, for a single second, looking at the fantastic molten candles of the island across the lagoon, it cannot be correct to say that he suddenly looked across at the mountains. It is truer to say, perhaps, that he woke up. The remarkable air of sightlessness in the very pale blue eyes was dispersed for a moment or two, enabling him to focus properly on something that it was now obvious he had not been seeing before.

He also pointed – with, I noticed, his scarless arm.

'At the end of the month I was over there.' He turned to me now, as he had done in the barber's shop, with the beginnings of a smile. 'I don't suppose you saw the schooner come in this afternoon? The one in the squall?'

'I did,' I said.

'That's the one,' he said. 'Takes four hours. That's the way you get there.'

3

The schooner, throbbing and rolling like a butter churn, loaded with everything from cows and bicycles to barrels of *vin ordinaire*, took him over to the island almost exactly a month after he had first arrived in Tahiti. By that time he had drifted into a habit of getting mildly drunk every night and sometimes also at the lunch hour: not because he particularly wanted to get drunk but because of all the pleasant pointless things there were to do this required least energy and passed most time.

As the schooner drew nearer to the island he gradually realized that the mountains he had previously seen only from a distance were really less like candles than gigantic chimneys, massed to the very ridges with vegetation. Their outline made a strange green graph, rising and falling violently, against the sky. Along the coast and a mile or two out from shore the reef was locked like a stupendous jagged collar on which the sea rode with unremitting roar, magnificently springing with high snow-white arches of spray.

After two or three stops at little village landing-places where boys sold him slices of frost-fleshed water melon on the quay-side the schooner finally ran, about mid afternoon, into a long still lagoon. He had already noted with some pleasure that the sand about the villages was white. Now the schooner began to run so near to the coast that he could have leaned out and thrown a stone on to the strips of pure white coral beach that ran everywhere out from thickets of bread-fruit, wild plan-tains, palms and the tall yellow-flowered hibiscus from whose bark the so-called grass for skirts was made.

The water in this land-locked lagoon was so still and undis-torted that it made him feel extraordinarily peaceful. In occasional shallow bays it was pure yellow in colour, turning to greenish blue, then pure bold indigo as the water deepened. The only disturbance on it was the wash of the schooner and occasionally, far off on the flat sun-white surface, a flight of little fish, pure frantic silver, scared from the water by some predatory chaser like a flight of birds.

His destination was the last stopping place but one along the lagoon, a wooden landing stage behind which was a solitary palm-thatched house and at the side of which stood, on stilts, in shallow yellow-blue water, what he took to be the rest-house. Like a fairly large square bamboo band-stand, it rose from the strip of pure white shore.

A boy of twelve came down from the house to greet him, to smile enormously and to take his bag. He stood for a moment in the glare of sunshine, waving his hand to the departing schooner. As it throbbed down the lagoon, farther into the intensely green shadow of the mountains, the sound of its engines dying away, he was aware of his sense of tranquility deepening. This is it, he started thinking, this is what I came to see.

Then, as he turned to go up to the house, an extraordinary thing occurred. Perhaps it was merely extraordinary, he explained to me, because he hadn't expected it. He had told no one he was coming there but now, as he turned, someone was waiting there to greet him.

It was a girl, holding an enormous crimson *lei* in her hands. He supposed, he said, it was the largest *lei* he had ever seen, a great flowery boa of petals minutely crinkled, so that they looked like feathers packed together.

But it was not this in itself that was remarkable. What immediately struck him as so extraordinary was that the girl, though quite young, eighteen or nineteen, was the ugliest he had ever seen. It was difficult to convey the peculiar quality of her ugliness but it was, he explained to me after several attempts, exactly that of a primitive idol hacked out of a golden-coloured wood, and not very well hacked at that.

She was so ugly, in fact, that she was, in a peculiar way, quite handsome. Her frame was tall and massive. Her bare feet were immensely broad and flat, with gripping toes. Her hands, which would have made a lesser *lei* look no longer than one of the necklaces of pink coral he had often seen in the shops, were like great golden-brown crabs with extended claws. Her legs, he said, were like those of a billiard table built in smooth shining mahogany and her arms, no less powerful, were as broad as hams where they joined the wide naked shoulders.

These were his own descriptions and he apologized for mixing them up a little but he went on to say that all the skin of her body was very fine, with a look of being oiled and polished. It was her face that had the rough-hewn look. The big dark brown eyes seemed not quite squarely fixed and the mouth seemed to have been plucked severely sideways and upward out of shape, curling the inner edge of the upper lip so that it looked like a half-healed scar. Later he saw in fact that it was a scar, as if at some time she had been violently struck across the face by a blow that had also flattened and broadened the square snout-like nose.

Crowning all this was a mass of overpowering jet-black hair that she wore unplaited. It was like a gigantic wiry horse tail that reached to her massive buttocks. Later she was actually to put on lipstick and an occasional bangle and sometimes a pair of ear-rings but that day the only decoration she was wearing was a large pure yellow hibiscus over her right ear. That too was an outsize flower, with a big stiff central pistil that stuck out at him like a darting tongue.

Her only garment was the *pereu* in the usual pattern of crimson and white, in this case of leaves and flowers, and it had been wound so tightly across her enormous breasts that she actually seemed to have outgrown it. It left all the upper part of her chest, her arms and her shoulders naked.

When she smiled at him the scarred lip seemed to give a raw flare and he saw that she had one tooth missing just underneath the twist of it, exactly as if knocked out by the blow that had caused the scar.

She placed the *lei* round his neck and greeted him, at first, in French.

'You don't speak English?' he said.

'A little.'

'And the boy?'

'My brother? Just little words of French.'

She led him up to the house. To one side of it, the shady side, a sort of bamboo and palm thatch lean-to hut had been built and there she showed him into a simple room where later he used to lie in bed and stare at the whole tranquil seaward stretch of lagoon.

He continued to speak in English, asking her one or two questions, such as her name and where he would be able to eat and so on, and every time she attempted to answer in English she gave a great crackling laugh, throwing back her head and opening her mouth to its widest, revealing her thick animal tongue stiff and quivering.

He could not quite grasp her Tahitian name. He thought it sounded, at first, like Tavae. He was not sure and tried to repeat it and she laughed again.

'They call me Thérèse too sometimes,' she said. 'Thérèse I like better.'

From that moment onwards he called her Thérèse. 'My name is Rockley,' he said. At first she pronounced it in the French way, as if it had an accent at the end, but later, as time went on, she simply called him Rock.

'Will you have something to drink now?' she said. 'Tea or coffee? Wine or coconut juice or orange?'

He thanked her, said he would have orange but that what he wanted to do most of all was swim.

'Good. You swim,' she said. 'I'll make orange and bring it down to you.'

'Good swimming?' he said. 'No sharks?'

'No. No sharks,' she said and she laughed, raucous, showing her tongue again. 'If sharks come I frighten them.'

He started to unpack his bag. She stood watching for a second or two, then said 'Please: excuse,' and started to go to the door. For so large a girl she moved with remarkable silence and it was several minutes later that he looked up, thinking she had gone altogether, and saw her still standing at the open door.

Then, for the first but not the last time, he got a totally different impression of her. The hut had only one small window so that it was fairly dark inside, and in the strong outside light she stood partly framed in shadow. He could not see the details of her face. She stood with one arm brushing back her hair, looking back at him, one leg crooked in an attitude of being arrested in a turn.

For a moment you could forget then, he said, how ugly she was. You could see how superbly and splendidly she was built. She made on him for a moment the same impression as an inanimate object, something magnificently executed: a well-made boat, an idol, a piece of sculpture, even a mountain.

'If you want something,' she said, 'you must ask me. Or Timi, my brother. Or my mother. How long will you stay here now?' He hesitated, more than anything because he was fascinated by the way she stood there, to all appearances ugly no longer, and she said: 'Oh! well, you tell me later. Doesn't matter. You stay one week – one year – two years!' and then she turned on her heel and went away with a curious massive gracefulness, laughing with throaty splendour.

There was just one more incident that stuck in his mind that afternoon before darkness fell. After he had been swimming for a good hour or more he came out and sat on the landing stage, deliciously wet and refreshed after the first swim he had taken.

Evidently she had been watching for this moment from the house, because a second later she was coming down to the landing stage with a pitcher of orange juice and a glass on a tray.

'You swim long time,' she said. 'You must be thirsty now.'

She sat beside him on the landing-stage and poured his drink. She sat with legs curled under her, watching him, pushing back her hair.

'You swim good,' she said. 'I swim every day too. Could you swim to the other side?'

He was still panting from exertion and was able, for a few seconds longer, only to shake his head.

'Sometimes I swim there and back,' she said.

'Oh! not me, not me,' he said. 'Too far. Out of practice.'

'Not so far.'

She laughed, enlarging her scar, and he sat drinking his orange juice, staring across the lagoon. Across the skin-smooth shadows, far off, a shoal of tiny fish burst from the water, as in the earlier afternoon, like fragments of silver. The crests of the mountains, far up, smouldered in sun. The deep far shadows under the thicket of the opposite shore grew greener and greener every moment, solid and glassy and finally untranslucent in the changing air.

He looked along the shore, tired but not too tired, blissfully and completely entranced by the tranquillity, the rapid embalmment of air and water and sky under approaching twilight and by everything he saw from the flaring tips of the mountains to the flick of a canoe paddle far down, seaward, towards the end of the lagoon.

Then he became aware, as he watched, of an unusual thing. In the afternoon, coming along by schooner, he had noticed the flowers of the tall grey-green hibiscus trees, those from the bark of which the so-called grass was made. Like soft pollen-dusty yellow cups they covered the boughs, the sand below the boughs and floated where they fell in water.

Now, to his surprise, the same flowers were red in colour. Both where they grew and where they fell they glowed in a shade of cinnamon, warm and deepening.

His surprise, when he spoke of it, made her laugh again.

'Every day they change,' she said. 'In the morning they begin one colour and as they die they become another colour. In the morning yellow. In the evening red. And then in the morning the new ones yellow again.'

And that, as he said to me, was how he felt about himself. Between morning and evening he had become a different person. It was unquestionable, he thought, that he had found there what he had come to see. And as he looked along the shore, where little fiery jungle cocks, quite tame, strutted scarlet and green about strips of well-watered grass, under palms and among crimson clumps of ginger-lily, he felt that everything was in perfect, ordered pattern, absolutely ordained and right from the changing colours of the hibiscus flowers to the crow of jungle cocks still giving to their hens among the tree-ferns fierce territorial warnings that hawks still hovered somewhere above the steely leaves of palm.

He was ready, he felt, to stay a million years. The pure absolute tranquillity had already started to hold him like a drug. He felt glad already of every breath of it. He was even glad of the big, overpowering, ugly girl who sat with him for nearly an hour longer, telling how she swam the lagoon, how she speared shrimps in fresh-water streams at night-time by shining a lamp into their eyes, and about the changing colours of hibiscus flowers: the soles of her big feet dark and horny like the feet of a bear.

4

He lived, for the next month, the happiest days of his life. The girl, the boy and her mother, a blousy, prematurely paunched woman who spent most of her time in the open kitchen-shed at the back of the house, looked after all his wants with tireless attention and yet left him free.

At the hotel he had eaten mainly European food, more French than anything in character, the sort of food he would have eaten anywhere, and he had liked it very well. Now he learned to eat, and also to like very much, mostly native food: dried raw fish, hot crabs, breadfruit, fried plantains, sweets of guava and coconut cream and curries of various kinds, including the delicate fresh-water shrimps found in the mountain streams. In a sort of dug-out at the back of the house stood a great barrel of *vin ordinaire* from which they drew him wine by the jug. He found it made him sweat a great deal but he drank it constantly.

Every day he swam, before and after breakfast, and then again in the afternoon and evening, half a dozen times between dawn and sunset. When he was tired of swimming he slept; when he was tired of sleeping he walked along the lagoon, either to-wards its land-locked end where a cluster of fifty or so dwellings lined the road, or seawards, where he could swim again or watch the Pacific hurling itself with its towering white horse waves against the reef, on one part of which, by the gap, the iron skeleton of a wreck stuck up as a mass of twisted junk, rust-orange through the glittering mist of ocean spray.

Occasionally he walked inland, climbing to the lower part of the foothills. In parts old plantations of guava trees had been felled to give more grazing for cattle; the grass was green and fertile. Great jungles of banana flapped overpoweringly above groves of orange and *pamplemousse*, the big pinkish grapefruit of which he never tired at breakfast. Narrow rapid streams watered pleasant little valleys of breadfruit, wild lime and avocado pear, and jungle cocks kept up their ceaseless crows of warning, invisible about the thickets, proud against hovering hawks.

Sometimes, this being the rainier season, it rained torrentially as he walked. He started by running for shelter. In a few days he was walking on through hot quick squalls, his shorts and shirt soaked, taking a bath as he walked. Sometimes, after these storms, he stripped out, hung his clothes on a rock in the sunshine, and swam naked while they dried.

Occasionally the girl came with him. Once as they walked together a sudden squall obliterated half the lagoon, flooding the sandy path under the palms to a depth of six inches. The faces, bodies and clothes of himself and the girl were sluiced as if under warm fire-hoses, so that when it was over she looked like some enormous water-animal that had just dragged itself, blubbering and dripping, from the sea. Then, her hair matted and drenched, the lines of her body more gross than ever under the soaked *pereu*, she looked even uglier than before.

There were two things, all this time, that he liked about her. He was fascinated, first, by her great strength; it impressed him enormously. And the other was, as he put it, that she didn't care a damn.

By that I thought he meant, at first, that she was very free, generous or in some way promiscuous. On the contrary, he said, the very opposite was true. She had a strange, proud, almost virginal sort of dignity.

What he meant, I gathered, was that she was a sort of tomboy. Perhaps, with her great strength, she would naturally have done nothing but heave boats about, swim the breadth of the lagoon, spear fish, roll barrels of *vin ordinaire* up from the schooner, and slog through the thickets with cordwood on her shoulders. His impression was also, since any girl looking into a mirror could hardly have failed to have grasped the ugliness of that kind of face, that she might have given up, as fairly hopeless, the idea that any man, drunk or sober, would find her attractive. Free of feminine obligations, as he saw it, she could behave before him with the physical ease, lack of embarrassment and sheer strength of another male.

She too swam a great deal. In the water, as in every other way, she was massive and powerful in all her movements. At the same time water gave her gracefulness. Wearing an ordinary two-piece swimming costume of black material she swam with superb and easy power, her long black hair trailing out like water-weeds.

One morning she challenged him to swim the breadth of the lagoon with her. He knew that his powers as a swimmer were really not up to this but she said:

'Swim slowly. You can do it. We can rest for an hour on the other side.'

To his surprise he made the opposite shore without much difficulty. He found that he was, in fact, in better physical condition than he had ever been. He felt taut, springy and in splendid shape all over. The wide Pacific air had given him an incredible feeling of buoyancy.

Then, as they swam back, he caught sight of a large indefinable underwater object rolling straight before him in the lagoon. Like a grey sloppy shadow, it made a huge rippling wave as it swam. He took one swift look at it, yelled, 'Sharks! My God, sharks!' and started to lash out in panic in the opposite direction.

He had no sooner turned than he heard her laughing. He turned back to see her waving a knife above her head.

'Ray! That's all!' she was shouting. 'A big ray. That's no harm. That won't hurt you.'

The giant ray, looking as he described it like some sort of indiarubber submarine, rolled ponderously off as he turned and swam back to her. The look of fright on his face must still have been remarkably vivid by the time he reached her because she burst out laughing a second time and said:

'Now you really look like a white man. Very white – *so* funny.'

He did not, he confessed, feel funny at all. He felt more than a little sick. His buoyancy had gone and his legs felt queer and shaky.

'You're not afraid, are you?' she shouted. She held up the knife above her head, cutting at the air with a slash. 'Shall I kill him? I can go after and kill him if you like. Shall I go?'

'Good God, no,' he said. 'Leave the damn thing and let's get out of here.'

'Funny! So funny,' she said.

Then as they swam back, he taking continually involuntary glances over his back to make sure the ray had gone, he said:

'I didn't know you carried a knife. I didn't notice that before.'

She turned in the water, swimming on her back.

'I keep it inside here,' she said. She tapped the folds of her costume about her enormous hips. 'I make a pocket inside.'

He knew that meant there must be sharks and he felt a little sick again.

'You never know,' she said. 'Shall I make a pocket for you? It's easy to sew one in.'

'So is sitting on dry land,' he said and at that she started laughing again.

It was his first and only swim across the breadth of the lagoon and he had to confess he hadn't liked it very much.

'At the same time, when I looked back on it,' he said, 'I got an odd comforting sort of feeling about it. There was nothing to account for it then, but I somehow got the feeling that if there had been trouble she'd have gone through hell to get me out of it.'

After that he kept his swimming to within short distances of the shore. When he wanted to cross the lagoon or change the monotony of swimming he took the outrigger canoe and paddled about instead.

Besides the little out-rigger the family had a large craft that carried a single sail. Most of their fishing was done with long five-pronged spears, sometimes at night, by the light of torches of palm-frond, or communal fashion, whenever a shoal moved up the lagoon. Sometimes these shoals took several days, perhaps nearly a week, to move the full length from the reef-gap to the last upper finger of shore. Then the great communal net was thrown out, to be drawn gradually about the shoal, in the upper narrowing reach of water, until the fish could finally be pursed and drawn ashore.

On the last day and during the last hours of this netting every villager, except perhaps a few Chinese share-cropping vanilla up the valleys, came down to help with the great task of pulling in the net. Men, women and children sat on the sand beneath the palms, chattering excitedly until the final hour when every hand was needed for the pulling. After that the catch was distributed communal fashion, according to degrees of labour, and men who had handled the net for days would find themselves with so much fish to spare that they could make it up for market in long strings, sending it over by the next schooner to Papeete.

About a month after Rockley's arrival on the island a shoal of great size, moving very slowly, came up the lagoon. It took several days to travel the three and a half miles of water. It was often difficult, Thérèse said, to gauge the rate at which a shoal could travel, especially a large shoal. There would often be days of tedium, false alarm, rising excitement and much tension before the net could finally be closed.

Rockley had greatly looked forward to helping at one of these catches but the shoal was so slow that on the fifth day he found himself, at midday, rather bored with waiting.

'It's always the same,' the girl said. 'It may be this afternoon. May be tonight. We have to have patience. We can never tell.'

Then he asked her if she would be going to the net that afternoon.

'I must go to the net,' she said. 'It may happen suddenly. If I don't help with the net I get no fish.'

Some time later, after she had served his lunch, he watched her going away to join the boy and her mother at the net. As she walked down the path she turned, waved to him and said:

'You sleep. When it's time I'll send Timi with a message. Then you can come down and you will have fish too.'

'How many do you suppose they'll give me?'

'Oh! plenty. Plenty for strong men. You must pull hard. I'll show you how to pull.'

He slept for a couple of hours, woke suddenly and went down to the landing-stage. Across the lagoon the boy was paddling shorewards in the outrigger. Rockley was sure the time had come for closing the net and that the boy had come to fetch him.

'Not yet,' the boy said. 'Long time yet. Perhaps tonight. Hours.'

Rockley sat down on the landing stage and watched the boy beach the outrigger. Then the boy climbed up on the landing stage too and they sat for a few minutes talking.

The afternoon, Rockley said, was very beautiful, with great clusters of sea-packed cloud on the mountains and a light of sheer purity, miraculously soft and limpid, across the glassy water. It was very hot and the fronds of the palms were so still in the heat that they looked as if scissored out of stiff green metal. The only sounds were the crowing of jungle fowl and, from so far off that they seemed strangely small and toy-like, the voices of villagers waiting at the net.

Suddenly he realized that for the first time, in the middle of this exquisite stillness, he was really bored. He had had his fill of swimming; he was tired of waiting for the shoal.

'I felt,' he said, 'as if I'd like a damn good talk to somebody. You know, a good yarn. In fact, to be honest, I was a bit lonely. I suddenly felt a hell of a long way from anywhere.'

Then he made, he said, the first of three serious mistakes. It was a very simple thing and at the time it seemed quite impossible that it could have, as casual things sometimes do, significant consequences.

Without thinking, he asked the boy if he would take him down the lagoon for an hour, in the outrigger, as far as the gap. The boy hesitated. He even looked, Rockley realized afterwards, a little uneasy, almost scared. Then he made various excuses, including the main one that the shoal might be landed at any moment, and Rockley said:

'Oh! Just half an hour then. After that I'll come back with you to the net.'

Distances by water are always deceptive and he had never really had to calculate how long it would take to paddle to the seaward end of the lagoon. It took, in fact, an hour; and then not quite an hour, because of a strong incoming drift, to paddle back again.

It was all so pleasant, unspectacular and dreamy between the walls of palm and the higher jungle thickets that he did not realize that the flowers of the big hibiscus were already turning from yellow to red by the time he and the boy were again opposite the landing-stage.

Then he saw the boy suddenly lift his head, brown eyes sharp and startled. From the upper end of the lagoon there was a deep murmur of voices. The boy started paddling furiously, quite agitated now, and Rockley knew that the final netting had begun.

By the time they reached the net, ten minutes later, the water at the end of the lagoon was like a white living cauldron of struggling fish. The boy was so quick to beach the outrigger and run along the shore that he actually tripped, fell and then rushed on, wiping his sandy hands on his bare thighs, quickly spitting on them afterwards.

Perhaps seventy or eighty people, Rockley said, were pulling at the net, and presently he found the boy, the mother and the girl among them. With her colossal mahogany legs locked in the coral sand the girl was not only pulling with all her enormous strength but with a remarkable expression on her face. Her dark eyes were large and blazing, with a peculiar fanatical light in them.

As he took up his place beside her, taking hold of the net, he had no idea that this in fact was anger.

'You said you would show me how to pull!' he said.

She did not speak. She neither turned nor looked at him. She simply stared at the net, the water and the leaping fish and lugged with all her astonishing strength at the net, her expression never altering.

He supposed, he said, that he must have spoken to her a dozen times or more that afternoon as they pulled together at the net, but each time she gave him no hint of a word or look in answer. It was pretty hot and strenuous work and he was glad when it was over. By that time darkness was falling and there were still some hours of work to do with the sorting, sharing and stringing of the fish. He knew that the stringing would in fact go on all night, so that the strings of fish would be ready for the incoming schooner on the following day.

Soon after half past six he started to walk back to the rest-house alone. As he was leaving the net he passed the girl, stopped for a moment and said:

'I am going back to the house. Will you be coming back?'
Again she made no answer.

'No need to come back for me,' he said. 'I can find a little fruit and eat that. Fruit and a little wine – that's enough for me.'

She had not even paused to listen and now by the time he had finished speaking she was already some yards away, striding strongly out of reach of him.

He went back to the rest-house, sat on the little veranda, too tired even to wash, and then drew himself a pitcher of wine. Then he sat on the veranda again, watched the stars in the lagoon and above the fantastic graph-like ridges of the opposite mountains and also the flares burning in a great cluster at the end of the lagoon.

Normally the wine, the evening, the stars and the mysterious waving half-drowned lights of the flares would have soothed him deeply. That evening, instead, he felt bothered – not worried, as he was careful to explain, but bothered – bothered, mystified and slightly irritated. He couldn't think what on earth he had done. The incident of the boy and himself going down the lagoon never occurred to him as the remotest possible cause of anger in anyone. He couldn't explain it at all.

Then, much later that night, he thought he caught a glimpse of what the causes might be. He woke about midnight to the sound of quarrelling. In the house the girl was reviling someone, with great fury, in words he didn't understand. He heard the boy's voice in answer. He got out of bed, went to the door of his room and listened. He thought he heard the sound of beating. After that he went back to bed, listened for a time and thought he heard an even odder sound – that of somebody weeping. But whether it was the boy or his sister crying somewhere outside in the darkness he never knew.

'Before I came down here I read somewhere,' he said, 'that these people were light-hearted, frivolous, courteous, generous but deceitful and cruel.'

He paused and before going on he gave one of those odd smiles of his.

'But that night,' he said, 'I started to find out they could be something else besides.'

5

Next morning, he said, it was impossible to recognize, or even believe in the existence of, the girl of the evening before. If the flowers of the hibiscus trees had been purple that morning instead of yellow the change could not, he said, have surprised him more.

She was smiling broadly as she brought him his breakfast of *pamplemousse*, coffee, fresh-baked Chinese bread and butter, boiled eggs and a basket of oranges, papayas, limes and avocado pears. She actually prepared the *pamplemousse* in front of him. Then she poured his coffee. Then while he was eating the *pamplemousse* she cut a large papaya in half and began to prepare it too, knowing he liked to finish his meal with that. In the bright orange cradles of flesh the black-grey papaya seeds glistened like fat beads of caviare.

All day she remained smiling, attentive, rather talkative and extremely sweet to him. There was no mention either of the incident at the net or of the boy. In the late morning she rolled up the skirt of her *pereu* above her knees, stood in a shallow part of the lagoon and washed her hair. Fresh-fallen hibiscus flowers floated on the water and under and about the landing-stage small fish of brilliant blue, with stripes of bright ochre, swam tamely in and out of the sunshine.

One of the pleasantest things about life there, he said, was to watch the Polynesian girls wash their hair. Its great length, its strong blue blackness and the way it glistened as it dried quickly in the sun were all beautiful things to see.

'I watched her half the morning,' he said. 'And she chattered as if she hadn't seen me for years.'

Soon it occurred to him that she was spending more time than usual on her hair, combing it and recombing it, shaking it out and spreading it over her shoulders to dry. At last he spoke about this, teasing her very slightly, and she said:

'Tomorrow night there will be dancing. Had you forgotten?'

Occasionally on Saturday nights young men and girls came up from the village, sometimes bringing a drum, a banjo and a guitar. There would be a good deal of wine-drinking, singing of songs, dancing, noisy frivolity and provocative laughter. A lot of flirting went on and the girls swung taut rubbery hips, their tight skin golden in the lamplight, and curled their fingers in subtle invitation, making the men excited. Most of them wore lipstick, generally of much the same carmine shade as the big hibiscus flowers in their hair.

The following night she too wore lipstick. It was, he said, the first time he had ever seen her wear it and it made a difference to her face that was sharp, uneasy and startling. He was not sure, at first, that it did not make her uglier than ever. The big mouth became more than ever like a scar. But the chief difference, he said, was that it gave her a sort of defiance, a certain touch of savagery that made her look out of place among the smaller, prettier girls.

That evening he danced with her several times and once or twice the banjo played European or American tunes. He drank a fair amount of wine, thought the stars of the southern hemisphere had never looked so huge, soft and flower-like above the lagoon and in general enjoyed himself greatly. She too seemed very happy. The most remarkable thing about her, he said, the thing that never failed to surprise him each time he held her in his arms for the dances, was the lightness of her enormous body. It was quite unbelievably perfect, he said, in its sheer balance and poise.

About midnight he walked outside to light a cigarette, relax a bit and get a breath of air. An exquisite little wind, heavy with warmth and tree perfume, blew for a moment or two across the lagoon, died suddenly and then sprang up again, stirring the fronds of the palms. He stood for a time under a palm tree and watched the stars.

He had drunk, he thought, quite enough wine, though not too much to prevent his remembering, after a few minutes, that he had been told not to stand, sit or lie under palms. Coconuts falling from a great height are projectiles of considerable nuisance and he laughed to himself as he remembered it and moved away.

Then the wind sprang up again across the lagoon, giving quite a gusty shudder in the fronds of palm, almost as if a storm were blowing up. He heard it stir the water, creating a sudden short rush of waves that lapped against the outrigger and rattled the boat chain.

A moment later he saw her come out of the house and down to the landing-stage. The fact that she went straight to the boats made him think that possibly she too had heard the stir of wind and had come down, as she sometimes did at night, to see that the canoes were safely moored.

She stood for some minutes on the landing-stage. In the rest-house the banjo and the drum were thumping with low regular rhythm, softly, and a long bar of light came from the open walls and across to the landing stage.

She stood just beyond the edge of this light, hands on her hips, looking at the water, and for some time he stood some distance away, uncertain whether to speak or not, watching her.

'Then I made another mistake,' he said. 'Another damn *faux pas*.'

It was four or five days after our first meeting that he got as far as telling me this and up to that time I hadn't attributed to him any great sense of humour at all, but now across his face there went, I thought, the flicker of a grin. A moment later I realized it wasn't a grin. It was a deadly stab of pain.

He walked over to where she was standing on the landing

stage. As she heard him coming she turned, moved a step or two and lifted her head. The light from the rest-house was shining behind her now and suddenly he saw her like a big muscular idol, all black except for pure edges of light glimmering along the massive curves of her shoulders, her thick upper arms and the fringes of her hair.

She looked exceptionally dark, powerful and magnificent. The individual features of her face were lost in shadow. All he could see was a great carved head, sharply poised, well up, with its flowing mass of hair. Then she moved again, her eyes glinted quickly in the house lights and he saw her shake back, with a splendid roll of her neck, one side of her hair, showing suddenly the bright yellow saucers of flower above her ear. He saw the sumptuous heave of her breasts and then suddenly, more than a little drunk, he forgot for the first time how ugly she was.

A moment later he was kissing her. Or rather, after the first impact of his lips, she was kissing him. As with everything else she did it was powerful and massive. It was an affair of overwhelming physical splendour. She gripped him with great strength, locking him against her passionately, and in a queer melancholy fashion repeating his name.

6

He realized, next morning, what a stupid mistake he had made. He only hoped she would forget it as soon as he wanted to do.

'The confounded trouble was,' he said, 'that I couldn't forget it. I'd really got quite fond of her – not in love or anything like that, but just fond, in exactly the same way as you get fond of a great big ugly dog. Except for her face there was nothing you couldn't admire and like about her. She was very, very likeable.'

And not only, as he explained, the girl. All of them were very likeable. The mother was eternally pleasant, smiling and soft-eyed. The boy was quick, good-looking, light in frame and surprisingly energetic. He was always fishing, making or mending the long elliptical baskets of bamboo for keeping fish alive and fresh under water, doing jobs on the boat or the outrigger. Occasionally Rockley helped him with these things.

After the incident of kissing the girl he began to welcome more and more the chance of slipping away to swim or fish with the boy. He welcomed a chance of mere companionship. That was one of the ways in which he hoped the girl would see that the affair of the kiss and what followed it was merely an episode he didn't want repeated. He was desperately anxious not to become involved in anything deeper.

'It had just the opposite effect,' he said.

Whatever he did with the boy aroused her to terrible silences: moods that lasted, sometimes, the greater part of a day. Two or three times the boy and himself took the outrigger as far as the seaward end of the lagoon but on the third of these trips she was so inexplicably sullen, black and mute against him that he was determined never to make one again.

Another day he and the boy walked up the mountainside, a distance of four or five miles, to where, on the edge of the thicket, eight or ten men were felling a tree for a dug-out canoe. He had very much wanted to see how these canoes were made and he spent a very pleasant day. After the tree had been felled and trimmed the men began the preliminary work of hollowing out the trunk with axes. After they had roughly shaped it, lightening it a good deal in the process, they would steer it, on rollers, down the mountainside. The whole business would take a week, perhaps ten days, according to the size of the tree.

It was very pleasant there in the brisker upper air of the mountainside, sitting under the shade of a big breadfruit tree, watching the men, quenching his thirst by sucking sweet oranges gathered from neighbouring trees and listening to the sound of a stream running down somewhere under a jungle of glinting elephantine banana leaves. Then as he watched the fresh golden bodies of the men sweating while they worked on the tree he remembered how he had once read, probably as a boy, how the North American had shaped his canoe by filling the hollow with water, throwing red hot rocks in it and thus giving it curvature.

It was all so interesting that he was glad he had taken his camera with him. It was the kind with the view-finder at the top. He took about a dozen pictures, first of the men working on the hibiscus trunk, then of various groups of them standing on or about the tree, then one or two of the boy, either alone or with the men.

Finally he decided he would like a couple of pictures of himself with the men. He had never let the boy use the camera before but the view-finder was so simple that it took less than a minute to show him how it was used. The boy was not merely delighted about this; he was innocently, worshipfully overjoyed. He fairly danced with the camera, Rockley said, so much so that finally Rockley had to leave the group and demonstrate how the boy must press the camera against his chest in order to prevent it shaking. He found then that the boy's hands were actually quivering, almost shuddering, with excitement.

There was a great deal of jollying, golden-bellied laughter about this and the boy responded by behaving, in a charming way, as if he were a person of singular privilege, almost a hero.

'It did your heart good to see him,' Rockley said.

Later in the afternoon, as he and the boy came down the mountainside, a single cloud on the upper crest of mountain enlarged itself, descended suddenly and broke in a storm. They ran for shelter in a shack owned by a toothless Chinaman who share-cropped vanilla farther up the hill. The rain, warm, steamy and torrential, beat into the great leaves of surrounding forest like a sluice while thunder walked up and down the dark precipitate valleys between strange fires of sun and lightning.

In the middle of all this the Chinaman hobbled out, bandy-legged, into lakes of rain, coming back some minutes later with half a dozen oranges and a spray of vanilla orchid and two vanilla beans. Rockley sat under the wide eaves of the shack and sucked oranges and watched the Chinaman explain, with neither French nor English but only little gestures of a pair of yellow dirty hands and a matchstick, how the cream lips of the little delicate self-sterile ghost-orchid had to be fertilized.

Presently the rain stopped as suddenly as it had begun and there was more laughter, very high-pitched and tinny, from the little Chinaman, as Rockley allowed the boy to take another picture of himself and the Chinaman standing by the door of the shack. All about them the forest sparkled and dripped with water. On Rockley's hands was a strange combined fragrance of oranges and vanilla, at once fresh and exotic, and he felt it had been an enchanted, exhilarating day.

'But that was only half what the boy felt,' he said. 'He was still so excited when we left the Chinaman that I hadn't the heart to take the camera away from him. I let him keep it slung round his neck and he went down the rest of the mountainside like a king.'

Then, as the two of them reached the rest-house, the boy started to run forward. He was twenty yards or so from the house when Thérèse came out of it. As soon as she saw him she stopped. He was still very excited, waving his hands about, making demonstrations with the camera and calling her name.

Then, four or five yards away from her, the boy stopped too. He flicked open the view-finder of the camera and started to look into it, laughing, as if about to take her picture.

'The next thing I knew,' Rockley said, 'was that she had snatched the camera from his neck and was swinging it wildly round her head, like a prehistoric sling or something, as if she was going to bash his brains out.'

The boy ducked in terror, put his hands up to his head to protect himself and then ran to the house. She took a dozen or fifteen furious bare-footed strides after him, screeching madly and still swinging the camera about her head.

It wasn't until the boy disappeared into the house that she seemed to come to her senses. Then her arms suddenly dropped. She stared in a stupefied sort of way at the camera, as if not sure now whether it was a camera or a sling-bag or something else and then came slowly back to Rockley.

'She just stood there, gave me the camera and stared,' Rockley said. 'No recognition in the stare. No contrition. No apology. Nothing like that. Just a long, empty, sightless stare.'

This episode perturbed him so much that he could not sleep that night. After some hours he got up, put on a pair of straw slippers and walked down to the landing stage. He started to smoke a cigarette and think things over. In the pure dark sky the stars seemed more brilliant, more beautiful and more voluminous than ever. He stared at them and their reflection across the lagoon for a long time and then, in spite of them and the pleasure everything about the place had given him, he came to a decision.

'I decided,' he said, 'to get out. The schooner would be arriving in a couple of days. I could catch it and go back to Papeete.'

There wasn't, he said, much reasoning about the decision. He still had several weeks of his leave to go. He disliked Papeete. The trouble was that he had begun to be much more than disturbed. He did not know why, but for some reason he had a queer, fatalistic feeling of impending disaster.

He had already started to walk back to the house when he saw her coming down the stone steps to the landing stage. She suddenly halted half-way up them. This time there was no light from the house behind her. She was simply a shape of vague patterns, her *pereu* hastily wrapped round her, under the brilliant stars.

He was determined that, this time, there should be no nonsense: no more kissing. He was perfectly sober this time, with no fancy illusions about anything, and he walked straight past her, not stopping or turning until he reached the top of the steps.

Then he spoke to her. 'Thérèse,' he said.

She neither turned nor spoke to him.

'Thérèse,' he said, 'I'm going away. By the next schooner.'

There was no sort of movement from her. She was simply an enormous shape carved out of the darkness.

'Good night,' he said. He had already turned on his heel and was walking away. 'I'll be going the day after tomorrow.'

'The schooner doesn't come until the day after that,' she said.

'All right. Good enough,' he said. 'The day after that.'

He walked on. She didn't speak again. He went on and into the house with a feeling of relief mingled with sudden wretched twinges of regret. There was absolutely no reasoning in his going; he did not want to go. But he was convinced, absolutely certain now, that it was the thing he must do.

But before the schooner arrived, three days later, something else happened. He made, he said, the third of his stupid mistakes about her.

7

He was determined to leave in the friendliest possible fashion. He even started to plan little gifts for everybody and for the first of the three days he behaved with polite neutrality. He began by avoiding the boy. He deliberately swam, fished, walked and idled about the place alone. Whenever the boy approached him he made an excuse about a book, a towel, a letter or something and went away.

The immediate result was, as he said, that she couldn't have been sweeter. She was her old friendly, laughing, almost frivolous self again. She prepared his fruit at table, made jokes as she watched him eat and threw back her head in gusts of superb sumptuous laughter.

It was only when the boy came into sight that her attitude

and her expression changed. Then she seemed to go blank before him. A sort of blight came over her. Every vestige of light and friendliness was suddenly extinguished. He began to understand then what was the matter with her. For the first time, fully, he realized how jealous she was.

'That was the Polynesian virtue the guide-books had left out,' he said. 'So jealous she couldn't bear to share me with the kid, her own brother. So possessive that she was frantic about a boy, another male.'

The second day, having put his finger on the cause of everything, he decided to keep himself more to himself than ever. As a result, after breakfast, he walked the entire distance to the point at the end of the lagoon. A white sandy track wound pleasantly under high palms past occasional abandoned gardens of half-wild gardenias, croton and tiare trees. A few wooden shacks, some empty, some with a few cockerels crowing about them, were dotted about the thickets. From far off came the inexhaustible thunder of the reef and then, at the very tip of the land, in from the open ocean, the great blown cloud of spume, white and glittering and sometimes rainbow-shot, in the brilliant air.

He was half-way back from the point when a voice hailed him unexpectedly from one of the houses in the thickets on the shoreward side of the track. He turned, stopped and saw a girl waving her hand.

'Hullo there,' she said in English. 'Good morning.' She was walking across the garden towards the thin cane fence that flanked the track. 'I thought it was you.'

He said good morning, staring blankly and did not know what to do.

'You're staying at the rest-house, aren't you?' she said. 'Don't you remember me?'

He said he was sorry: he didn't remember.

'I saw you quite a few times at the New Pacific Hotel,' she said. 'Dancing. Over at Papeete.'

'Oh! yes,' he said.

'I really come from here,' she said. 'I go over for a few weeks sometimes.'

She smiled: uncommonly small, pale and compact, with a delicate upward cast in her eyes that he afterwards knew came from the mingling of Polynesian blood and Chinese. She moved with grace. Her voice was soft and rather high. To look at her after looking at Thérèse was, he said, like looking at a little yellow parakeet after a buzzard, or at one of the little angel-finned blue-and-ochre fish after the giant sloppy ray that had scared him in the lagoon.

'Like it here?' she said. 'I saw you go past once before, but you were with Timi that time and I didn't like to call.'

'I like it very much.'

'How long do you think you'll stay?'

'As a matter of fact,' he said, 'I'm off tomorrow. Catching the schooner.'

'If you like it so much why are you off tomorrow?'

It was altogether too complicated to explain and he said he didn't know.

'Catching the next plane?'

'No,' he said. 'The one after.'

'You look hot,' she said. 'Wouldn't you like to sit down on the veranda a minute and I'll get you something to drink? Some lime or orange – whichever you prefer.'

A few moments later he was sitting down on the veranda of the little house. Going in and out of the house, getting his drink of orange, she moved with pert grace, not wearing the ordinary *pereu* but a simple waistless dress of yellow with several circles of emerald at the edge of the skirt, her dark hair plaited.

'Pretty as hell,' he said. 'But then, no point in describing her. You've seen her already. That was her outside the barber's shop, that time you first met me.'

He stayed for another hour. She lived with a mother, three elder sisters and an aunt, but that morning they were up at the plantations of vanilla, some way in the hills, fertilizing flowers. It was a job, she explained, for which the big Polynesian girls were far too clumsy but which the delicate fingers of Chinese or part-Chinese did rapidly, skilfully and with perfection.

He could not help being fascinated by her own thin delicate hands as she sat there telling him these things.

'Don't you work in the plantations too?' he asked her.

'Not often,' she said. 'I look after the house mostly and do the cooking. I have a little trouble with my heart sometimes. Nothing much, but the hills are too far for me.'

She put her left hand on her chest, just above her heart, and held it there. She was wearing in her hair not the big customary hibiscus flower but a little cluster of *tiare*, not more than six or seven blooms of small wax-white stars. Her breasts were sharp and upstanding, her arms were almost pure ivory, the nails shapely on the fragile little fingers, and he could smell the fragrance of *tiare* in the air.

The following day the schooner sailed without him.

8

Thérèse was delighted by his sudden change of plans. During the next few days, as she sat about the place at the various tasks of grating coconut, crushing herbs, preparing breadfruit, topping and tailing shrimps, washing and drying her hair, he knew that she was very happy. He heard her singing a good deal. He would not have been surprised if her voice had emerged as a baritone but it was in fact a rather thin soprano, high and pure. The songs she sang were repetitive, a little melancholy and mostly fairly slow and dreamy, like lullabies. A few weeks before he would have asked about these songs and perhaps have got her to tell him the meaning of the words; but now he was wary of doing anything, even in the most casual way, that she might interpret as affection.

For this reason he made a series of excuses for getting out of various things she wanted him to do. He had, for instance, asked several times about fresh-water shrimps and how she caught them at night, in the little streams, by the light of flares. For some time he had wanted to go on one of these shrimping expeditions but now he made excuses of some sort whenever she mentioned it.

Soon she began to grow more and more persistent about this. In fact, as he said, she started pestering.

'Why don't you come with me? You say you want to come. All the time you say you want to come with me and now you don't come. Why won't you come?'

He would make some excuse about being too tired at night or the wine making him sleepy; or he would change the subject completely.

'I'd rather go fishing for tuna,' he would say. 'Out in the open ocean. They fight so much better than shrimps do.'

This, though it made her laugh, did nothing to stop her persistence.

'We can do both,' she said. 'Tonight we can catch the shrimps. Tomorrow we can take the boat and catch tuna.'

He wanted, in fact, to do neither. What he chiefly wanted to do now, and he found it more attractive every day, was to walk along the lagoon to the house among the thickets and play, as he put it, with the little paraqueet there. The little paraqueet was, it seemed, amusing in many ways. Her heart, not quite strong enough to stand work in the vanilla plantations or the gradients up into the forests, exercised itself freely in other directions. On hot still afternoons he lay for hours on the beach with her or on a cool truckle bed inside. Paraqueets, as he explained, are extremely affectionate creatures. They are also very teachable and quick to learn. And sometimes darkness was already falling when he walked back to the rest-house along the lagoon.

Then, when he got back, Thérèse would say:

'You walk a long time, don't you? How far do you walk every day?'

'I like to look at the wreck,' he would say, 'and wonder how it got there. I like to watch for tuna. I thought I saw tuna leaping yesterday.'

All this time he was afraid she would be suspicious. To his relief and surprise she was not suspicious: not, at any rate, at first. She seemed absolutely content, perfectly happy, simply to have him there. It was enough, it seemed, that he hadn't gone away.

Then, after about a week, she said:

'Don't you get tired of watching the wreck? Soon I shall begin to think you go there to look at something else besides.'

'Such as what?' he said. 'It's beautiful. I like looking at the ocean. I saw a little plane yesterday.'

'Such as the little Chinese girls in the house along there,' she said. 'They're very beautiful too, the little Chinese girls.'

For the moment it was on the tip of his tongue to say that the house was always empty when he passed it, but he saved himself in time.

Even then there was no sign of her suspicion. There was not the faintest hint of jealousy. At the same time he felt disturbed. Women, as he remarked, are not compared with cats for nothing. They have infinite capacities for awaiting their time to strike. Gossip, moreover, is the fastest traveller in the world.

He decided, as a result, to go with her on the night-shrimping. That, he thought, would be the clever thing. That would appease her.

They set off the following evening at nine o'clock. The nights were always infinitely beautiful, full of a humid and fragrant softness, under enormous stars. But that night, under dense thickets of hibiscus and breadfruit that overhung the bed of the little stream, the boughs touching overhead in the narrow valley, most of the stars were hidden. He had always thought of the sky, especially that brilliant southern sky, as a companionable place, and that night, under the thick forest leaves, he missed its brightness. As a result he got an increasing sense of uneasiness. There was something uncanny about it all.

Most of the time she walked in her bare feet on the stones of the stream. In her left hand she carried a torch, an ordinary electric battery one, and in her right a thin two-pronged spear. Soon he was watching her shine the torch into little beds of shrimp eyes: the eyes, he thought, like imploring guileless little beads, full of wide and dark surprise, as they looked up to their death-blow.

For about an hour he and the girl walked up the narrow valley. During this time he carried the basket and sometimes he could hear the faintest rustle, a mere papery whisper, as the still-alive shrimps stirred among each other in the darkness.

Finally they came out into a break in the thickets. It was a grassy place, with a number of rocks strewn about it, and he sat down on one of the rocks, putting the basket at his side.

A moment later, in a sudden turn, she shone the torch into his face. 'Oh! accidentally, of course,' he said, 'but for a moment I was half blinded and I couldn't see. You know how it is – your eyes feel stabbed and they start throbbing up and down.'

Then, as his eyes cleared, he saw her standing above him. Whether it was quite accidental again he never quite knew, but he could have sworn the spear was poised. She stood there exactly as if preparing to strike him, just as she struck the shrimps, between his dazzled eyes.

He supposed it must have been accidental, a mere slip of her hand, because a second later she put out the torch and dropped the spear on the ground. She was kneeling in front of him, grasping his hands.

'Please,' she started saying. 'Please, Rock, don't go away. Please.' Her voice had a desperate unnerving break in it. 'You won't go, will you? When you said you would go I thought I would go mad. Quite mad. I couldn't speak about it before, but don't go, Rock, will you? Please don't go.'

As she spoke she drew herself up on her knees, until her face was level with his. Her voice was so uncertain that he actually thought she was sobbing. Even in the brilliance of starlight he was not sure whether her enormous eyes were dry or not. He only remembered with a sudden stab of panic, the night when he had kissed her and had forgotten for a moment how ugly she was.

'Thérèse,' he started saying. 'Look –'

'You could like here. I can build a house. I will build a house and live like your *vahine*. It cost nothing. I'll be your *vahine* and work for you. I'll work for you and you can love me –'

He listened, amazed and at first absolutely speechless. Embarrassed too, he actually managed to stand up without seeming to push her away. A moment later she stood up too, suddenly pressing her body against him, her great arms seizing and holding him in a vice.

'Listen to me,' he started saying again. 'Listen –'

Before he could go on she started kissing him. There was no escaping the big scarred mouth and she was so violent he could not resist her.

'I might just as well have resisted a buffalo,' he said. 'And I believe she might have killed me if I had.'

He admitted, in fact, an extraordinary thing. He was afraid of her, he said, really quite afraid. He feared her physically.

Then, a moment or so later, a curious change came over her. She seemed to go suddenly limp. She let her hands fall loosely at her sides and she sat down on one of the rocks, quietly.

This quietness of hers was so sudden and so complete that it unnerved him as much as her violence had done. She sat staring heavily into the darkness and for about five minutes he stood there watching her. All he could hear was the noise of the stream falling away over its stones among the thickets and the small whisper of shrimps as they rustled in the basket.

Then she started speaking.

'Rock –'

That was as far as she got. Her voice was constricted. The one word was almost a cough.

Then after several more minutes she tried speaking again. By this time her hair had partly fallen over her face and she did not brush it away.

'Rock,' she said, 'I –'

For the second time she couldn't go on. She put her hands on her knees, gripping them, and her hair fell still further forward over her face, almost hiding it completely.

'What were you going to say?' he said.

She gave a great sigh, more like a sudden gasp for breath, and then violently locked her hands together.

'Nothing,' she said. 'Nothing, I –'

'What was it?' he said.

'Nothing,' she said. 'I was thinking –'

She suddenly leapt to her feet, stumbled forward and started clumsily to walk down the mountainside.

'What were you thinking?' he said. He picked up the basket and started after her. 'What was it?'

She didn't answer. It was some moments before he caught up with her, crashing heavily down the mountain path.

'Thérèse,' he said. 'What was it? What were you thinking?'

She crashed on through the thickets, making no attempt to stop or look at him. She blundered forward like an animal that had lost its way. But what really disturbed him was not that, he said. What affected him so much was the enormous and helpless sorrow in her voice when she spoke again.

'Thank God,' she said, 'my thoughts are my own.'

9

He had already made, by that time, the third of his mistakes. He determined not to make another.

'I got the thing taped up,' he said. 'I found you could pick up the schooner at a village on the other side of the island. In fact on schooner days and on Saturdays there was a bus that would take you there. The bus actually came by the rest-house, used the track along the lagoon and went round the island by way of the point.'

Two or three days before the schooner was due he started to get a few of his things together. He would pack them up a few at a time and then, when the girl was down by the landing stage, gutting fish or getting water or washing her hair, walk along the track to the house in the thicket and leave them there. Fortunately he had only one bag and after two or three journeys most of his things were with the parakeet, under the truckle bed.

'I know it probably sounds pretty ungrateful and all that. I wanted to do the decent thing but I could see trouble everywhere,' he said, 'if I didn't get out. Besides, what do you say? If you're going to live with one of these girls you might as well pick a good looking one. A parakeet. Not that I wanted to. One way and another I felt I'd had about enough and a bit over.'

As he said this he gave me another of those dispirited, rather twisted smiles of his.

'And I was just about as wrong about *that*,' he said, 'as I could be.'

Then, on the morning of the day before the schooner was due to arrive, he began to have something approaching misgivings. He felt very sad. He had not only loved it all. It was, as he was never tired of saying, the most beautiful place on earth. The lagoon alone, sheltered and guarded by these fantastic palm-fledged mountains behind which every evening the sunset opened up like a blast furnace, flaring with every colour of flame, was paradise itself.

'They say that the original Garden of Eden was here somewhere in these islands,' he said, 'and my guess is this was it.'

All this, together with his thoughts of how nice the people

183

had been, how tranquil and serenely restful it all was, were enough to explain his sadness.

'I could have wept,' he said. 'In fact I was so damned miserable that when she suggested, that morning, having a trip for a few hours to look for tuna I jumped at it like a shot.'

Then, at the last moment, when the boat was ready, he remembered being alone with her twice before, once on the landing stage and once on the mountain, and he didn't fancy it a third time.

'Let the boy come, won't you?' he said. 'He loves the boat. He handles it well too. Go on – let the boy come.'

The boy was standing on the landing stage, watching his sister and Rockley prepare the boat. He gave an eager glance at her as Rockley spoke. For a moment she hesitated. Then she gave one of those strong sudden twists of her neck, threw her long hair back from her shoulder and said an odd thing.

'If he likes to take the risk,' she said.

At once the boy clambered down into the boat and in five minutes they were sailing seawards down the lagoon on a light warm breeze. Rockley steered, the boy handled the sail and Thérèse squatted in the bows, busying herself with lines and the long white-feathered spinners they were going to use for lures. Rockley noticed that she didn't speak much, though once, when they were almost level with the house where the parakeet lived, she turned full round, faced him and said:

'Wouldn't you rather be walking instead?'

He didn't pay much attention at the time. No one was moving outside the house. He couldn't help wondering what might have happened if the parakeet had suddenly come out, recognized him and waved her hand but nothing happened and the boat sailed tranquilly past the house and the thicket of breadfruit and hibiscus with their pretty scatterings of fallen flowers.

After a time he became more and more aware of the growing thunder of the reef. At the mouth of the lagoon, still a mile or more from the gap, it was already like the battering surge of an enormous waterfall. He was surprised, even at that distance, by the height of the breaking spray and the strength of the tow pouring in through the gap. Beyond it the Pacific looked calm enough, a brilliant slaty blue without so much as a single white crest across it, but he was to discover only a few minutes later that it was really corrugated by deep, long and powerful swells.

Meanwhile the boy took in the sail and Thérèse started to steer, calling to Rockley at the same time to take a paddle. For another twenty minutes he and the boy paddled towards and finally through the gap. It was hard going and once or twice they seemed, he thought, to be making no headway at all against the power of the tow. On both sides the reef rose like rough brown jaws, the coral clear of water, the rust on the wreck glinting scabbily with the colour of old dried blood, in the iridescent sunshine.

By now he was paddling so hard that he had no time even to brush the sweat from his face. He simply let it pour down over his eyes and lips and into his open mouth, the rivulets of it gathering on his neck and chest and pouring down his body. Then his legs began to feel soggy. He was sucking his breath in short desperate gasps. Then he felt the boat give a sudden twist, almost a whip to starboard, and he saw the boy ease his rate of paddling.

Less than a minute later the sail was up again and they were well clear of the reef, out in the open sea.

After the exertion of paddling he felt considerably exhausted: so much so that for a time he paid very little attention to either the girl, who was steering now, or her brother, who once again was handling the sail. He thought he heard her occasionally giving directions to the boy about a change in course but now she spoke in Tahitian and he was not quite sure. He actually shut his eyes for a moment or two. Then he was sharply woken out of himself by a sudden brittleness in her voice, a hard rasping shout, and he opened his eyes to see her hauling on the thick

185

stumpy rod from the bows, her enormous forearms locked stiff with the pull of the line.

A few moments later the first tuna was thrashing about in the well of the boat. It wasn't very large and the girl, as if angry or disappointed about its size, suddenly picked up a short stump of wood and started clubbing it to death. She hit it so severely that it actually gave a shocked sort of leap a foot or two in the air and blood spurted everywhere, spattering her bare feet and shins and over her forearms and hair.

Then she whipped out a knife. It was the same knife she had brandished above the giant ray in the lagoon. It was short, thick and slightly curved.

She bent, a moment later, over the dying fish. She lifted the knife quickly as if she were going to plunge it into the short, iron-smooth body. The boy was at the sail, his back turned.

Rockley waited for the downward cut of the knife. Instead he saw her stand up to her full height. She stood there for a second or two before he realized that her face suddenly looked uglier than ever. He didn't quite grasp it at first. It was evil and dark and the lip was grossly twisted.

Then she gave a grotesque short yell.

'You go to that house!' she yelled. 'You go to that girl. You're going away with her. I saw you take your things. You go to that house, don't you?'

She made a powerful lunge at his face with the knife. He instinctively put up a hand to protect himself and he felt the knife run in a hot sharp line down his outer forearm. He staggered for a moment and the boat started rocking. He was aware of her making a second lunge. She looked queerly unkempt and wild now, her face frighteningly ugly, her black hair sweeping about her hips and blood spattering her legs and arms, and she started yelling again, the words incoherent this time.

The boy too stood up, relinquishing his hold on the sail. He shouted something too, at the same time trying to grab at her arm. She moved so quickly, stabbing air, that he missed her completely, overbalanced and himself made a grab at air.

A moment later the spar, swinging round, struck the boy full across the mouth. He fell like a boxer, backwards, eyes wide and cast upward, stunned before hitting the water.

10

In a flash the girl stooped, picked up the bloody slithering fish in her arms and hurled it over the stern. A moment later she was swimming.

The boy had already disappeared. And for the space of what seemed to be several minutes, though it could not have been more than a moment or two after she dived, Rockley was alone on the sea.

In the confusion he had fallen on his knees. Now he tried for several seconds to get up again.

His arm was drenched in blood. He tried to clutch the side of the boat with his good arm and then, already fainting, with the other. Then his head fell on his arms and blood started spewing over his face and shirt and body.

He came round to find himself hanging over the side of the boat, down which blood was flowing into the sea. He was too weak to do anything for a moment or two but presently he managed to heave his legs upward until he was half on his knees again. Then with his good arm he staggered struggling to drag his shirt over his head.

The shirt was half-way off when he heard the girl shouting. His head was trapped, as it were, in a crazy sort of bag. From a distance her voice sounded unreal and hoarsely muffled. After a second or so he managed to drag the shirt free of his head and then, his eyes woken suddenly by the dazzle of sunlight, he saw the girl.

She was already hanging on to the side of the boat, holding the boy. She was thrashing water violently with her legs and trying at the same time to heave the boy with her enormous arms and shoulders out of the water. It was as much as Rockley could do to crook his good arm over the side and shout for the boy to clutch it. He was relieved then to see the boy shake his head, quickly shut his eyes and then as quickly open them again.

A second or two later the girl gave a tremendous heave and the boy fell face forwards into the boat. As he fell over the side he knocked Rockley, too weak even to kneel now, on to his back. Rockley groped there for a moment, blood pouring down his arms and mingling with tuna blood, and then managed to raise himself on one hand, partly supporting himself on one of the paddles.

He was still struggling up when the girl started screaming. The boy yelled, whipped the paddle suddenly from under Rockley's knees and started madly thrashing water. All the time the girl continued screaming, trying at the same time to heave herself into the boat by her hands.

It was not more than five minutes, Rockley said, at most ten, before he and the boy somehow pulled her aboard. It seemed, he said, like a day. After a time she stopped screaming. Her great scarred mouth folded itself down until the lower lip was invisible and her teeth, clenched far below it, were actually drawing blood.

She still had so much strength that, even then, at the very last moment, she made the final effort of pulling herself aboard. Her entire body seemed to retch itself into the boat with a terrible groan.

She lay there for a minute, perhaps longer, face downwards, before Rockley realized that what he thought was merely the tangled mass of her water-soaked *pareu* folded like a twisted red sheet about the right side of her body was really all that was left, on that side, of her thigh. The teeth of the shark had scoured deep into flesh, so that the bone stared blue.

She somehow turned herself over on her back, still conscious. Rockley picked up his shirt, throwing it over her thigh.

Faintness started a second wave of blackness across his eyes and by the time he had defeated it he was aware of the boy using his own shirt to bandage his arm.

Some time later the boy had the sail up again and the breeze, blowing crossways towards the reef, began to take them back to shore. All the time the girl lay starkly conscious, her big hands gripping the sides of the boat in stiff agony, her teeth biting lower and lower into the jaw.

For most of the journey back he was simply unaware of the sea. Once or twice he fainted off again and then he was aware, presently, of kneeling beside her, smoothing her hair with his good hand. There was nothing else he could possibly do for her and it was some time before there was even a hint of conscious recognition in the enormous eyes. Then quite quietly, and with a strength of tone that almost fooled him for a moment into thinking that he was, after all, merely on the fringes of a dream of pure ghastliness, she said:

'I'm glad you're with me.'

He could find nothing to say in answer. It was actually the first time her mouth had relaxed, allowing the teeth to give up the cruel biting of her jaw. Almost at the same time, as if she had suddenly defeated all pain, her hands relaxed too, unlocked themselves from the side of the boat and folded themselves weakly across the front of her body.

'Rock,' she said, 'let me hold your hand.'

For a long time she held his hand while keeping her eyes fixed on his face. 'I'm sorry about the other hand,' she said once and again he could find nothing to say in answer except, so long afterwards that it was merely like an echo that had lost itself across the space of sea and had in some uncanny way floated back again:

'I'm sorry too.'

Half an hour later they were running through the gap. All this time he had been so unaware of both time and distance that he actually saw the reef before being aware of the thunder of its roar about him. In the same way he had forgotten the boy, sitting all the time like a strangely aged little statue, all splashed with blood, never speaking, in the stern.

As they drew into the calmness of the lagoon she actually smiled up at him, held his hand a fraction closer and spoke for the first and only time of the parakeet, the other girl.

'I found out last night,' she said. 'I saw you go there. Then I knew you had been there before.'

It would have been better, he said, if she had stuck the knife into him after all.

'I couldn't sleep last night. Then I came and looked at you while you were asleep,' she said. Her voice was proud and without scorn. 'And I knew you were going away from me.'

Now they were running quite fast into the lagoon. He stared away from her towards the thickets beyond the white strips of beach, hot in the sunshine, and to the rising tiers of palm.

'I said I wouldn't let you go away from me,' she said.

He looked back at her face. Its sudden relaxation after pain into calmness made it appear, quite suddenly, not so large as before. The lips were more compact. Even the big snout-like nostrils seemed to have contracted.

'Now when you go away from me it won't matter.'

He could find nothing to say.

'I told you my thoughts were my own,' she said. 'Do you remember?'

Her voice was very low. He still could not speak or look at her and all his pain and fondness for her dissolved into sudden desolation. He was aware of nothing except a long, profound, tormenting anguish before, for the fifth or sixth time, he fainted away.

When he looked at her again her eyes were staring straight up into glaring sunshine. Her face was no longer placid. In its final moments, no longer ugly, it seemed to have expanded again with remarkable strength, defiantly. With pride she seemed to be glaring back at the flaming sky, handsome and almost contemptuous as she lay there.

A moment later he covered her face. The boat ran past the house in the thickets, where the little parakeet lived, and all across the lagoon the crowing of jungle cocks was proud and clear.

H. E. Bates in Penguins

DEATH OF A HUNTSMAN

'He has few equals among writers currently working in England or America . . . Each of these situations is worked out with delicate skill, each scene is set with easy cunning; the jovial businessmen on the five-ten that takes them to their valuable, lossmaking farms; the brassy heat of the little Spanish port; the brooding strangeness of the house the lorry-driver finds himself in by accident – all this is brilliantly done' – John Metcalf in the *Sunday Times*

This is the latest among many books by H. E. Bates to appear in Penguins. Those at present available include his uproarious stories of the Larkin family:

THE DARLING BUDS OF MAY
A BREATH OF FRENCH AIR
WHEN THE GREEN WOODS LAUGH

and his famous wartime novel:

FAIR STOOD THE WIND FOR FRANCE

NOT FOR SALE IN THE U.S.A.

For a complete list of books available please write to Penguin Books whose address can be found on the back of the title page